Suddenly Sienna turned back to the car.

'Did I drop a pen in there?' she asked, leaning in over the door. Her hair, loosened by the wind on the drive, slipped out of its knot and fell forward around her face.

Jason's pulse sped up. *Friends!* he thought. *Who am I kidding?* She was searching the seat, but she soon found her pen and looked up. Jason stared at her lips, slightly parted, then raised his eyes to meet hers. She held his gaze and didn't move away. Without meaning to, Jason found himself leaning toward her . . .

His lips were barely an inch from hers when the phone rang.

VAMPIRE
BEACH

Don't miss any of the titles in this edgy series:

Book One: Bloodlust

Book Two: Initiation

Coming soon:

Book Three

VAMPIRE BEACH

Initiation

Alex Duval

RED FOX BOOKS

VAMPIRE BEACH: INITIATION
A RED FOX BOOK 978 1 862 30197 9 (from January 2007)
1 862 30197 2

First published in Great Britain by Red Fox,
an imprint of Random House Children's Books

This edition published 2006

1 3 5 7 9 10 8 6 4 2

Papers used by Random House Children's Books are natural, recyclable products
made from wood grown in sustainable forests. The manufacturing processes
conform to the environmental regulations of the country of origin.

Set in 12/16pt Minion by
FalconOast Graphic Art Ltd.

Red Fox Books are published by Random House Children's Books,
61–63 Uxbridge Road, London W5 5SA,
a division of The Random House Group Ltd,
in Australia by Random House Australia (Pty) Ltd,
20 Alfred Street, Milsons Point, Sydney, NSW 2061, Australia,
in New Zealand by Random House New Zealand Ltd,
18 Poland Road, Glenfield, Auckland 10, New Zealand,
and in South Africa by Random House (Pty) Ltd,
Isle of Houghton, Corner Boundary Road & Carse O'Gowrie,
Houghton 2198, South Africa

THE RANDOM HOUSE GROUP Limited Reg. No. 954009
www.kidsatrandomhouse.co.uk

A CIP catalogue record for this book is available from the British Library.

Printed and bound in Great Britain by
Cox & Wyman Ltd, Reading, Berkshire

For L.A.'s finest writing group –
Chris, Drew, Emily, Kathy and Matt

Special thanks to Laura Burns & Melinda Metz

ONE

'Hey, Freeman! Wait up!'

Jason Freeman grinned as his friend Adam's voice carried across the wide-open courtyard of DeVere High. He turned, and found himself staring into a camera lens. Adam Turnball jogged toward him, jostling his ever-present camcorder as he filmed.

'I haven't been getting the hand-held camera effect I want in my film,' Adam explained. 'The camera's not shaking enough, so I'm thinking I must walk very smoothly. I'm extremely graceful, you know.'

'Hence the jogging?' Jason asked.

'Yeah.' Adam turned off the camera and bent over, sucking in a long breath. 'I tell you, bro, I suffer for my art. Running is not my strongest subject.'

Jason chuckled. He rarely understood what Adam was talking about, but he always found the guy amusing. 'I don't even think that thing's switched on half the time,' he teased him. 'You've been making this movie

1

ever since I met you and so far, apart from some party footage, I haven't seen squat.'

Adam fell into step beside Jason as they made their way toward the parking lot with the rest of the juniors and seniors who could drive. 'Let me guess: you think I use the camera as a shield between myself and the harsh realities of high-school society. That I don't feel safe without a camera. That I'm only comfortable viewing the world at a distance, through a sanitizing camera lens.'

'No, actually, I think you just like to freak people out by pretending to film them all the time,' Jason replied.

'Damn, you got me.' Adam grinned. 'But you know I always like footage of you. The Michigan farm-boy wholesomeness, the all-American blond good looks. Why, you could be the next Brad Pitt, my friend.'

'I've never set foot on a farm in my life,' Jason said. 'I'm from a suburb of Detroit.'

'Details.' Adam waved his hand dismissively in the air, his hazel eyes twinkling.

As they passed through the tall arch over the entrance to DeVere High, Jason took in a lungful of the warm California air. The scent of flowers mingled with the smell of the ocean half a mile away. Sometimes he still couldn't believe he lived in Malibu now. It had

2

been several months, but the place hadn't lost its ability to wow him. 'I can't believe it's November and I'm still wearing Tevas,' he commented. 'Do you have any idea how cold it is in Michigan right now?'

'Too cold for me,' Adam said. 'Anything below sixty-five qualifies as freezing as far as I'm concerned.'

'Hey, Freeman,' Brad Moreau called as they passed him. 'Turnball.'

'What's up?' Adam replied.

Jason nodded at Brad, his best friend on the swim team. But he didn't head over to the carved stone bench where Brad sat. Because Brad wasn't alone; he had Zach Lafrenière with him. And Zach was radiating 'no humans allowed' vibes that could probably be felt on Mars.

'What's with the vampire conference?' Adam asked, lowering his voice. 'Something going down I should know about?'

'You shouldn't know about any of it,' Jason muttered. 'And neither should I.' That was the single most astonishing thing about Malibu so far: the fact that the coolest kids in school weren't your usual 'cool' kids. In fact, they took 'cool' to a whole new level!

They were vampires.

Most days, Jason expected to wake up and realize

that half his new friends being vampires was just a bizarre dream. But so far it hadn't happened. Adam was the only other person he knew who understood the truth about Zach, Brad and the rest of that posse. And Adam didn't seem to find it nearly as freaky as Jason did.

But then, Adam had grown up with the vampires. And Jason had only met them a few months ago. Maybe over time, he'd get used to knowing such a massive secret. Maybe.

'Let's just go,' he said gruffly, wanting to change the subject. The way Zach looked at him made him nervous. Of all the vampires, Zach was the only one who put Jason on edge. The others mostly acted like normal – normal for SoCal – people. But Zach was different. More powerful. More reserved. And definitely more unwilling to befriend Jason – or probably any human.

'Aren't you going to wait for Brad?' Adam asked.

Jason shook his head. 'We don't have swim practice today. Coach Middleton said since it's a holiday week, we could have the time off. He figured nobody was going to be at their best two days before Thanksgiving.'

'Sweet,' Adam said appreciatively. 'Hey, that means we can hang after school tomorrow, right? I've been meaning to force you to watch the entire *oeuvre* of

Stanley Kubrick, a subject in which your knowledge is sorely lacking.'

'Hey, I've seen *The Shining*,' Jason protested.

'That's not enough,' Adam told him. 'What do you say – a DVD marathon *chez moi* tomorrow?'

'Sure,' Jason told him. They'd reached the parking lot. He nodded toward his 1975 Volkswagen Karmann Cabriolet, parked under a palm tree to the right. 'I'm that way.'

'And I remain in the bike parking section,' Adam said ruefully. 'Not that I don't love my Vespa. I just wish it had, you know, four wheels and a backseat to make out in.' He held up a fist, knuckles out toward Jason.

Jason bumped fists. 'Later.'

Adam took off for the Vespa with a wave, and Jason headed for his car. He wondered where his younger sister, Danielle, was. He'd forgotten to tell her there was no practice today. He could've driven her home. But a quick scan of the parking lot revealed no sign of Dani. She must have caught a ride or taken her usual bus.

'Guess I'm flying solo,' Jason murmured, unlocking the car. He began to lower the roof; it was way too sunny and gorgeous to ride with the top up.

'Want some help?' a voice asked from behind him.

Jason recognized that voice: *Sienna*. He felt a rush of

nervous energy – *that* was just one more thing he'd got used to. Sienna Devereux made him hot, she was a vampire, and she was taken. Strangely, perhaps, he was having the most trouble with that last one.

He didn't turn around. 'I've got it, thanks,' he said.

Sienna didn't leave. He laughed and glanced over his shoulder. 'You're not really here to offer help, are you?'

'Nope,' she said, her plump lips curving into a smile. 'I'm here to ask for some. Can you give me a lift home?'

Jason finally turned to look at her full-on. Man, she was sexy. Her dark eyes were gleaming with amusement, and her long black hair was pulled into some kind of messy knot on top of her head. Jason longed to pull out the pins that held it up and let her silky hair spill down over his fingers. He shook the thoughts away. She was Brad's girlfriend. He was Brad's friend. That meant that most interesting thoughts about Sienna had to be banished from his mind.

She and I are just friends, he reminded himself. 'What's wrong with the Spider?' he asked. Sienna's imported Alfa Romeo always seemed to be out of commission.

She shrugged. 'I think it hates me.'

'That's impossible,' Jason replied. She raised one perfect eyebrow, and he realized that he sounded like a complete dork. 'Cars don't have feelings,' he added quickly. 'Unless you know something I don't.'

'I know *lots* of things you don't,' she said lightly. She opened the passenger door and folded her long legs into the VW.

'So I guess I'm giving you a ride home.' Jason laughed. He hooked the folded top into place and climbed in beside her. 'Why don't you just get a new car? Your parents have the money.'

Sienna turned in her seat to look at him. 'Really now, Michigan,' she purred. 'If I had a new car, I wouldn't need rides home, would I?'

'My point, exactly,' he told her.

She shook her head, smiling. 'Well, where would be the fun in *that*?'

Jason grinned and found himself gazing directly into her beautiful dark eyes. Then he realized he'd been staring at her for just a bit too long.

Sienna leaned toward him. Close. So close Jason thought she was about to kiss him . . .

In fact, she gave his Michigan State key chain a casual flick with her finger. 'I think you have to use the little metal thingy on the end of this in order to make the car go,' she teased.

Jason turned the key in the ignition, trying to shake

off the feeling that something had just very nearly happened between him and Sienna. 'Ha! Like you'd know,' he retorted jokingly. 'Your car *never* goes.'

As he pulled out of the parking lot onto the Pacific Coast Highway, he caught a glimpse of Brad and Zach still sitting on the bench outside school. 'Why didn't you just wait for Brad to take you home?' he asked Sienna.

She didn't answer, and for a moment he wondered if she'd even heard him. He shot a glance at her, and she was frowning.

'He had to . . . do something with Zach,' she finally replied.

Jason nodded. It was just like he'd suspected. Brad and Zach were busy with some vampire-related business. Sienna didn't want to be specific about it, and that was OK with him. When he'd first found out about the vampires living in his gated community of DeVere Heights, he'd got pretty involved, pretty fast. One of them had turned rogue and killed a girl from school. Jason had ended up tracking him down and fighting him, all alone, in an alley. It had been that or let another girl get murdered.

If Zach Lafrenière hadn't turned up at the last moment, Jason knew he would probably have ended up dead. The whole experience had taught him everything he needed to know about the vampires: they were outrageously strong, they could change their physical appearance, and they knew some seriously freaky fighting moves.

He wasn't anxious to get that up close and personal with vampire business again. Being friends with some of them was enough – Sienna and her best friend, Belle, Brad and his oldest friend, Van Dyke. Even Zach was OK. Jason felt that they were good people and he knew their parents did a lot of charity work in the community. Beyond that, he didn't want to know much about the day-to-day vampire activities. His own private don't-ask-don't-tell policy.

A light turned red in front of him, and Jason eased to a stop. To the left, the Pacific Ocean spread out to the horizon, its gray-blue water calling to him. Maybe he'd slip on his new wetsuit and try some surfing this evening. Now that it was getting toward winter, the sun went down early. But he'd discovered that surfers stayed on the water until the very last drop of light was gone. He would definitely have time to catch a few good waves. He'd only taken three lessons so far, but he already knew enough to go out on his own.

The late afternoon sun glinted off the water, and a

warm breeze ruffled his hair. It was hard to believe it was almost Thanksgiving. Warm sun, clear blue sky, crashing ocean surf – life just did not get any better.

'You are seriously zoning,' Sienna commented.

The light was green. 'Sorry,' Jason replied as he hit the gas. 'Sometimes the whole Malibu thing still distracts me.'

'What "whole Malibu thing"?' she asked.

'You know, the unrelenting incredibleness of the place.' That was the best way he could describe it.

'Yeah. I've been to a lot of places, and Malibu is still the most beautiful,' Sienna agreed.

Jason glanced at her in surprise. Sienna's family – in fact, all the vampire families – had more money than he could even imagine. When she said she'd been to a lot of places, he believed her. The Devereuxs vacationed in Europe, Asia, even Australia. He'd seen the photos scattered around their house. It was nice to know that California still held up, even with that kind of competition.

'Any big plans for Turkey Day?' Sienna asked as they turned off the highway and headed up the hill toward DeVere Heights.

'The usual: lots of food, football on TV,' Jason told her. 'My Aunt Bianca is coming in from New York.

Danielle has about thirty outfits lined up to run by her. She approves of Bianca's fashion sense.'

'Well, who wouldn't?' Sienna said. 'The woman knows how to dress.'

Jason's eyebrows shot up. 'You know my aunt?'

'Sure.' Sienna gave a languid shrug. 'I mean, it's not like we're best friends or anything, but I've met her. Her husband was on the hospital board with my mom.'

'Oh.' Jason knew that Aunt Bianca had helped his father land his new job at the Los Angeles advertising firm – the new job with the huge raise that had led to them moving out here to Malibu. And he knew that Bianca had suggested they buy a house in DeVere Heights. But somehow he hadn't realized that Bianca knew Sienna and her parents. 'I guess Bianca's husband was really involved in all the Malibu charities and stuff, huh?' he asked.

'Yeah.' Sienna glanced over at him. 'Didn't you know that?'

'I never really thought about it,' Jason said. 'Aunt Bianca was only married to him for four years before he died. And it's not like they spent much time in Michigan – they were always off in New York or L.A. or Paris or someplace else exotic. I met him at their wedding and maybe once or twice after that.'

'So he wasn't exactly Uncle Stefan,' Sienna guessed.

'I guess he was, technically,' Jason said. 'I just never thought of him that way. We've seen a lot more of Bianca since he died than we ever did before. I think my mom is happy to have her sister back.'

'Makes sense,' Sienna said. 'But you should be glad Bianca was married to Stefan. If it wasn't for that you wouldn't be living in DeVere Heights.'

'What do you mean?'

'Bianca used his contacts. You know, pulled some strings for you guys,' Sienna explained. Then she grinned. 'We don't let just anyone live up here, you know,' she teased.

'So if it weren't for Uncle Stefan, I never would have met you,' Jason said. 'I guess I do owe him one, then.' *Was that too much?* he wondered the second the words left his mouth. Sienna always seemed to be flirting with him, but he didn't usually flirt back. He mostly figured that she was just kidding around.

Sienna didn't answer, but she gave him a long sideways look that sent the blood racing through his veins. Jason turned into the driveway of her ultra-modern house and stopped the car.

'Thanks for the ride,' she said casually, climbing out and closing the door behind her.

12

'No worries.' Just having her out of arm's reach made Jason relax a little. Sometimes it was hard to remember that they were only friends when she was so close by. He reached for the gearshift, but suddenly Sienna turned back to the car.

'Did I drop a pen in there?' she asked, leaning in over the door. Her hair, loosened by the wind on the drive, slipped out of its knot and fell forward around her face.

Jason's pulse sped up. *Friends!* he thought. *Who am I kidding?* She was searching the seat, but she soon found her pen and looked up. Jason stared at her lips, slightly parted, then raised his eyes to meet hers. She held his gaze and didn't move away. Without meaning to, Jason found himself leaning toward her . . .

His lips were barely an inch from hers when the phone rang.

Jason jumped in surprise as a Backstreet Boys song played out from his cell. 'Dani's idea of humor,' he explained to Sienna. 'She's always changing the ring.' He dug in the front pocket of his jeans and eventually managed to extract his phone, but he didn't recognize the number on the screen. He hit 'Talk'. 'Hello?' he barked into the mouthpiece. This was the worst-timed call he'd ever had.

It was too late. At the other end the caller had already hung up. Jason shrugged and turned back to Sienna.

But she was gone.

TWO

Not even the perfect Malibu sunshine could cure Jason's bad mood as he drove home from Sienna's house. He'd been so close to kissing her. He could practically feel her lips on his.

What kind of idiot answers the phone at a time like that? he thought, pulling to a stop in front of his house. *Why didn't I just ignore it?*

He pulled in a deep breath, trying to achieve calm. Sure, he'd been stupid to go for the cell. If he hadn't, he could have done what he'd been wanting to do for months – kiss Sienna. But she was Brad's girlfriend, and Jason wasn't the kind of guy to go around kissing his friend's girl. It would have been wrong. And obviously Sienna thought so, too, or else she wouldn't have taken off.

Maybe she was insulted that I answered the phone instead of kissing her, Jason thought. *Maybe that's why she left.* But he didn't think that was it. He figured she'd realized what they had come so close to doing, and so she'd left. She didn't want to hurt Brad anymore than Jason did.

With a sigh, he climbed out of the car and made his way into the house. It still shocked him that they lived in a place at least twice the size of their house back in Michigan. Sometimes it didn't seem possible that this was home now. But the delicious scent of his mother's pumpkin pie wafting from the kitchen sure made the place smell like home. Mrs Freeman had been making it every Thanksgiving since Jason could remember.

'Hey, Mom, I'm back,' he called, making his way into the kitchen.

'Good, you can help me,' his mother replied. 'I can't reach the good china; it's up on the top shelf.'

Jason shook his head. 'It's only Tuesday. Why are you getting the good china out now?' he asked. 'Thanksgiving doesn't start till Thursday, you know!' His poor mother looked ready to drop from exhaustion. Her blond hair was a mess, and her Mr Bubble T-shirt was covered with flour.

'You know I need to feel like everything's ready,' she replied. 'Just because it's a new house doesn't mean the Thanksgiving rules change.'

'Yeah, and the rule is that Mom has to be completely freaking out for the entire week before Thanksgiving,'

Dani put in from her perch on one of the stools at the breakfast bar. 'Why are you home so early?' she asked Jason.

'No swim practice today,' he replied, reaching over his mom's head and pulling down a stack of china plates. 'Sorry I forgot to tell you. I would've given you a ride but you were already gone.'

'Maria drove Kristy and me home. She got her license last weekend,' Danielle said. 'Isn't that cool?'

'Sure. It means less time as the Danielle taxi service for me.' Jason took down the gravy boat and handed it to his mother.

Dani ignored him. 'Anyway, on the way home we stopped at Peet's Coffee and Maggie Roy was there. She said Zach Lafrenière is having a huge party Friday night. It's his eighteenth birthday.'

'Huh,' Jason said. He realized that that was probably what Zach and Brad had been talking about at school. He had to smile, thinking how he'd assumed some top secret, hush-hush vampire business was going down when really they were just planning a party.

'You're going to go, right?' Dani asked.

'I guess. First I've heard about it,' Jason said.

'Well, Jason might be going, but you aren't,' his mother told Dani.

17

Danielle's mouth dropped open. 'You are *not* going to keep me away from the best party of the entire year!'

'Oh, yes I am,' Mrs Freeman replied. 'You know how I feel about DeVere Heights parties. The kids here seem to have a new one every week, and you tell me every time that it's going to be the best party ever.'

'Yeah, but this one really will be,' Dani argued. 'Tell her, Jason.'

Jason shrugged. 'Zach is the most popular guy at school,' he told his mom.

'Make that the most popular guy on the face of the planet,' Dani elaborated.

'Then I'm sure he won't miss you at his birthday party,' Mrs Freeman said to her daughter. 'He'll have plenty of friends to help him celebrate.'

'But—'

'No, Danielle. It scares me too much. I don't even really like Jason going,' Mrs Freeman said. 'Not since that yacht incident.'

Dani fell silent for a moment. Jason knew she'd been as freaked as he was by what happened at Belle Rémy's yacht party a few months back. That was when Carrie Smith had fallen overboard and washed up on the beach the next day, dead. Jason remembered it all too well – he'd been the one to find the body.

Mrs Freeman had pretty much changed her party-going rules a minute later. And she didn't even know the truth about what had happened at the yacht party. If she did, she wouldn't have stopped at keeping Dani home from the parties, Jason thought. She probably would have covered his little sister in bubble wrap and locked her in her room for a few years! Or, more likely, insisted that the entire family pack up and move back to Michigan. Because the dead girl hadn't drowned the way everybody thought. Carrie had been killed by Luke Archer, a rogue vampire who had sucked Carrie dry.

That was Jason's introduction to the vampires – a murderer on the loose, filled with a bloodlust that drove him mad. Sienna had told Jason that it was forbidden for a vampire to take the life of a human. And Zach had ended up killing Luke in order to stop him from murdering again. Jason believed them when they said there would be no more murders. When they said the DeVere Heights vampires only took a little blood from their human friends.

But that didn't mean he was OK with it.

Every party he'd gone to in DeVere Heights was an orgy of vampire feeding. The vampires supplied plenty of alcohol and some seriously upscale surroundings. And then they made out with whatever humans were interested – and given the glamour and charisma of the vampires, that was an awful lot of humans! In the process, the vampires drank human blood. But the humans never noticed. They barely even remembered. All they knew was that they'd had an amazing time – partying.

Jason knew how it felt. He'd been fed on by a vampire named Erin Henry. And he'd been deliriously happy for hours afterward. A little chemical bonus. If they could put that feeling into a pill, the world would be addicted. It hadn't hurt, and he knew Erin needed to feed in order to live. He understood all of it. But he still didn't want to be a vampire's dinner, and he didn't want his sister to be, either.

'Jason, are you going to help me out here?' Danielle asked, breaking into his thoughts.

'Uh . . . no,' he said. 'Sorry. Those parties do get wild.' *And you might get sucked on*, he added silently.

Dani rolled her eyes. 'I can't believe this. You've all turned into a bunch of conservative little grannies.'

'Well, that doesn't sound like much fun,' said a gravelly voice from the hallway. Jason turned to see his Aunt Bianca pulling a rolling suitcase in from the front door.

'Bee!' Mrs Freeman squealed, sounding just like

Dani when she greeted one of her friends. She ran over and threw her arms around her sister.

Dani laughed, and Jason knew why. Aunt Bianca was definitely not a 'Bee'. Bee was a cute little girl with pigtails. And Aunt Bianca was, well, stunning. She was tall and slim, with straight dark hair that hung down her back, and big, deep blue eyes. While Jason thought his mom was pretty – in an all-American mom sort of way – he knew Bianca was the real beauty of the family. It didn't hurt that she was wearing an all-black outfit with a knee-length trench coat and high-heeled black boots. She looked like she'd stepped out of a fashion magazine. He had no idea what label it all was, but he knew it must've cost a fortune. Maybe if his mom put on those boots . . . but Jason couldn't even imagine it.

'Hey, big sis,' Bianca said, hugging Mrs Freeman. She pulled away and looked her up and down. 'You look exactly the same.' Bianca glanced over at Jason and Dani and gave them a grin. 'But these two have gone California on us! Jason, I've never seen your hair so blond.'

He went over to kiss her hello. 'It's the sun,' he said. 'It's *always* sunny here.'

'So you like Malibu?' she asked.

'Definitely.'

'He fits right in,' Danielle added, coming to greet Bianca. 'He's already learning to surf.'

Bianca laughed. 'And how about you?' she asked Danielle. 'Are you adjusting?'

Dani shrugged. 'I have a few friends.'

'You have about twenty friends,' Jason corrected her.

'Yeah, but who knows how long I'll be able to keep them if I'm never allowed to leave the house!' Danielle replied, with a pointed look at their mother.

Bianca raised her eyebrows. 'Does this have anything to do with the old grannies comment?'

'You showed up in the middle of a battle. Clash of the generations,' Mrs Freeman explained.

'She won't let me go to a party—' Dani began.

'But we're not going to bore you with the details,' Mrs Freeman interrupted. She turned back to Bianca. 'How long are you in town?'

'A week or two,' Bianca replied, taking a seat at the breakfast bar.

'Are you going to see any movie stars?' Dani asked. Aunt Bianca worked as a casting director and frequently dealt with big-name actors. Even though she lived in New York City, her job required her to fly back and forth to Los Angeles several times a year. She even kept an office in L.A.

22

'I might,' Bianca said, her eyes twinkling. 'In fact, it would be helpful if you could come along and act as my assistant at some of the meetings.'

'Oh my God! I would *love* to,' Dani cried. 'Thank you.' She threw her arms around Aunt Bianca, and Jason felt himself relax a little. Two minutes with Bianca and Dani's foul mood was already gone. Jason was glad their aunt would be with them all weekend – it might even mean he would manage to get to Zach's party without a major scene from his sister.

'So when do I get the grand tour?' Bianca asked when Dani released her. 'I hope you guys like the house. Stefan always said DeVere Heights was the only place to live in Malibu.'

Mrs Freeman smiled sympathetically. 'It's your first Thanksgiving without him,' she said softly. 'How are you holding up?'

Jason knew that Bianca and Stefan had fallen in love pretty much at first sight. Even though Stefan had been a good twenty years older than Bianca, she had been completely and genuinely devoted to him. Jason had to admit that the few times he had met Stefan, the guy certainly hadn't behaved like a sixty-something. He was handsome, intelligent and witty and Bianca had taken his death – in a nasty traffic accident – pretty hard.

Bianca's smile faltered. 'It's tough, Tania,' she admitted. 'But being here with all of you really helps.'

Mrs Freeman nodded. 'Well, let's show you around, then.'

Jason grabbed his aunt's suitcase. 'I'll put this up in the guest room,' he said. 'I don't need the tour.' *What I need is some time to get over my idiotic behavior with Sienna,* he thought as he headed for the stairs. He had a feeling it wouldn't be easy. He might have to start with a long, slow lobotomy.

'I'm going to start you off with the worst one, just to get it over with,' Adam said after school the next day. 'Now I want you to be prepared. It's bad. It's very, very bad.'

'Then why do I have to see it at all?' Jason asked. He swung his locker door shut and took a moment to silently appreciate the lack of textbooks to drag home. Thanksgiving weekend equaled no homework. It would be nothing but fun for the next four days. Fun and food.

'Even the worst Kubrick is better than ninety per cent of the crap that most people like,' Adam replied. 'Besides, there's an orgy in *Eyes Wide Shut.*'

'Why didn't you just say so?' Jason joked. 'There's no

such thing as a bad orgy.' He led the way out to the front courtyard. A few guys were playing Frisbee on the lawn, and there was a mini traffic jam near the gates from the parking lot to the road. Everybody wanted to get out of school and start enjoying the holiday weekend.

'Freeman!' Michael Van Dyke came charging past, smacking Jason on the shoulder as he ran. 'See you Friday.'

'Zach's birthday soiree?' Adam asked, watching Van Dyke sprint for his Hummer. 'You going?'

'I guess,' Jason replied. 'Brad and Sienna both told me I *had* to go.' In fact, that was the only thing Sienna had said to him at all today. She hadn't exactly avoided him, but she also hadn't made eye contact even once. Was she thinking about their near-kiss from yesterday? Was she *relieved* that it hadn't happened – or disappointed? He couldn't tell. But if he went to Zach's party, at least he'd have another chance to talk to her.

'You think it'll be a typical vampire-fest?' Adam asked, lowering his voice.

'I'm expecting a little more from Lafrenière.'

'Fair enough.' Adam grinned. 'But I don't need anything fancy. Cold beer and hot girls, that's it!'

Jason knew the vampire parties could be relied

upon to provide all that in style. And this being Zach's eighteenth birthday bash, who knew what other amusements might be served up?

Although, Jason reflected, he'd be even more psyched for the party if he didn't know that the humans would be part of the buffet. There was something unsettling about it. Even with the whole no-harm-no-foul set-up. And even though Sienna and Zach had assured him that there were no other vampires who would succumb to bloodlust, he had a hard time letting go of his suspicion. Who knew what made a vampire cross the line? Maybe it was like becoming an alcoholic. Suddenly a couple of drinks just weren't enough. Suddenly one little drink of blood would lead to more and more and—

'Jason, look out!' Adam cried.

But it was too late. A strong arm wrapped itself around Jason's neck.

THREE

Jason's ju-jitsu training kicked in and, without a second thought, he grabbed the guy's forearm, yanked down, and at the same time threw his own weight forward. The guy stumbled to the side, releasing Jason to regain his own balance.

Jason immediately fell into a fighting stance. He remembered all too well what it was like to fight a vampire with superhuman strength. He had to be ready . . .

'Dude, chill!' his opponent cried.

Jason squinted into the bright sunshine, trying to make out the guy's face. 'Tyler?'

'This how you California guys say hello?' Tyler laughed, holding up his hand for a high five.

Jason laughed in amazement to see his old friend standing there. 'What are you doing here?' he demanded, slapping Tyler's hand.

'Visiting. Duh,' Tyler said cheerfully.

Jason shook off his surprise, reached out and hugged the guy. He hadn't seen Tyler in months.

'Somebody wanna explain all this male bonding?' Adam asked.

Jason stepped back and grinned. 'Adam Turnball, Tyler Deegan.'

Adam held out a hand. 'First friend in Malibu,' he said.

Tyler shook. 'First friend in kindergarten,' he replied.

Adam whistled. 'You totally win. Although Jason and I don't throw down every time we see each other.'

'Yeah, what was that about?' Tyler asked, rubbing his arm as he turned back to Jason. 'You're pretty twitchy for a mellow California dude.'

'Sorry,' Jason said. 'I was just thinking . . . Well, I, uh, got into a fight a while ago and when you grabbed me . . .'

'Say no more. I will not try the sneak attack hello on you ever again.' Tyler glanced around, his brown eyes wide. 'The guy in the 7-11 gave me directions to the school, but I thought he must be wrong. This place is awesome!'

'You're not kidding,' Jason agreed. 'The cafeteria has an ocean-view terrace.'

'You mean you don't have that in Michigan?' Adam teased. 'Do you at least have a *glacier*-view terrace?'

Tyler snorted. 'It's cold, but it's not *that* cold. Can't compete with this, though.' He glanced around again, and Jason took the opportunity to check out Tyler's jeans and well-worn Detroit Pistons T-shirt. He had a dark blue hoodie tied around his waist and his curly dark hair was longer than Jason had ever seen it. He also had at least three days' worth of stubble on his chin.

He looks like crap, Jason thought with a twinge of concern for his old friend.

Tyler turned and caught him staring. 'Admiring my new tat?' he asked, lifting his arm to show off a tattoo of Tweety Bird in garish yellow.

Adam laughed. 'What'd you do, hit the gumball machine?'

'You know it,' Tyler said. 'This was my prize. And there was a little kid watching, so I had to put it on.' He rubbed at the temporary tattoo with his finger. Tweety's face didn't budge. 'I can't get the damn thing off.'

Jason had been friends with Tyler long enough to know when he was putting on an act. And right now, he was acting like he was going for an Oscar in 'funny and normal'. But the stubble and the long hair and the showing up randomly in California – they definitely *weren't* normal.

'Where's your gear? Let's get it in my car. Or did you drive out here?'

Tyler held out his thumb.

'You *hitched*?' Adam yelped. 'All the way from Michigan?'

'Yep. I caught a ride with this one dude I know who took me through three states – a trucker,' Tyler said. 'Then I just hitched the rest of the way. I'm short on cash, so no first-class flights for me.'

'You're here. That's what matters,' Jason answered.

'I figured I'd crash your Thanksgiving. I couldn't stop thinking about your mom's pumpkin pie. It's like I could smell it from home and it just lured me out here. Think your parents will mind?'

'They'll probably kick me out of my room and give you my bed!' Jason said, slapping Tyler on the back. 'They love your ass.' Jason knew why Tyler didn't want to do the holiday thing in Michigan. His parents had divorced a year or so before, and it had been nasty. Now it was just Tyler and his dad in the house, and Jason knew things weren't too happy. No pie there.

Maybe a turkey TV dinner. 'There's plenty of room,' Jason added. 'Our new place is pretty big.'

'Understatement. His house is ginormous,' Adam volunteered. 'He's just being modest.'

'That's my boy,' Tyler replied. 'Freeman has always been impressively self-deprecating.'

Adam waved his hand dismissively. 'It's all an act,' he joked. 'What I find impressive is thumbing your way across half the country. That's a lost art, my man. Very Kerouac of you.'

Tyler shot Jason a questioning look and Jason laughed. 'Pay no attention to the Adam-isms. Half the time nobody really knows *what* he's talking about.'

'And that's just the way I like it,' Adam agreed. 'It keeps people off-guard. So listen, Jason and I were heading to my place for a movie-viewing plus pizza-snarfing party. You in?'

'Sounds good,' Tyler said. He clapped Jason on the back and headed off with Adam as if they'd been friends for years.

It's good to see him, Jason thought, smiling as he watched his old friend. He realized Tyler hadn't said anything about gear. The guy didn't even seem to have a backpack. Jason figured he must have left in a hurry.

He hoped it wasn't because things were bad – well, even worse than usual – at home.

'You wanna tell me what the hell that movie was supposed to be?' Tyler asked on the way home from Adam's that evening.

'Who knows?' Jason replied. 'Adam says Stanley Kubrick is the greatest director of all time and his movies are required viewing, even the bad ones.'

'Huh.' Tyler thought about it for a moment. 'People in L.A. are clearly bizarre.'

'Can't argue with that,' Jason agreed. *And Tyler doesn't even know about the vampires!* he reminded himself. The image of Sienna's face leaped into Jason's mind, and he shoved it away. He'd got used to doing that since he'd met her. But it was harder than usual today, because of the memory of the kiss that didn't happen. 'Hey, when did you leave Michigan?' he asked, forcing his mind away from Sienna. 'Why didn't you call me before you turned up?'

'I did,' Tyler said. 'I thought you Californians all had your cell phones surgically attached to your ears, but you didn't even pick up.'

Jason took the turn through the tall iron gates of DeVere Heights. 'When did you call?'

'Just yesterday,' Tyler said. 'Thought I'd give you a heads up, but when you didn't answer I figured I'd just surprise you.'

I can't believe it, Jason thought. *Tyler is the one who called when I was about to kiss Sienna.* Somehow, it always seemed to come back to Sienna. 'I didn't get to my cell in time, sorry,' he said. 'And I didn't recognize the number. It wasn't the Fraser area code.'

'Yeah, I got a new cell,' Tyler told him. 'It's from where my mom lives now, in Chicago.'

'You've been staying with your mom?' Jason asked, surprised.

'Nah. I went to see her a couple of months ago, but she was mostly busy with her new boyfriend.' Tyler drummed his fingers nervously on his lap, and Jason could hear the bitterness in his voice. Tyler still hadn't forgiven his mom for leaving. 'But hey, she sprang for a brand-new phone and I don't have to pay the bills. So it's all good.'

Jason didn't know what to say. Obviously it *wasn't* all good. But they were Tyler's issues to deal with, and he didn't want to make things any harder on his old friend.

Tyler let out a long sigh and leaned his head back against the seat.

'How long have you been on the road?' Jason asked. 'It must've taken days to get here.'

'Only two days,' Tyler said. 'I got lucky. Guess I don't look so much like a serial killer that people won't pick me up.'

'You look more like a serial killer than usual,' Jason told him with a grin. 'I know Coach Salzman isn't letting you in the pool with that hair.'

'Nah, I quit the team,' Tyler said. 'The relay was lame without you, anyway.'

Jason was too surprised to answer. He and Tyler had been on the swim team together since seventh grade. He'd known things were kinda bad with Tyler lately, but he never thought the guy would change *that* much. Although ... Jason couldn't stop himself from thinking about what had happened the last time he saw his friend. When the Freemans had left Fraser, Tyler had been pretty messed up.

'I know what you're thinking,' Tyler said.

'What are you, psychic now?' Jason joked.

'No, I just know you. You're thinking about what happened,' Tyler said. 'At your going-away party.'

'Yeah.' Jason slowed as they approached his street. 'Well ...'

'Look, I screwed up,' Tyler said. 'I know I did. But I

didn't think . . . I mean, I thought I could still show up and you'd be happy to see me. Am I wrong?'

'Of course you're not wrong,' Jason replied. 'But you took my car, man! You went joy-riding in my car while you were stoned. You could've totaled it – or, even worse, yourself or somebody else.'

'I know, but I didn't,' Tyler said. 'I'm fine, the car was fine, and nobody else got hurt. It was a stupid thing to do and it will never happen again. OK?'

'OK,' Jason replied, feeling relieved to have got that little issue off his chest and sorted out. He pulled to a stop in the driveway and turned off the engine. The house glowed welcomingly in front of them, its lights shining brightly against the dark November sky. Dani paced back and forth on the porch, talking on her cell phone. None of them got very good reception inside. 'This is it. *Mi casa es su casa* and all that,' Jason said with a smile.

Tyler reached for the car door handle, then hesitated. 'I just want you to know . . . I don't hang with those guys anymore – the ones I brought to your party. And as for the drugs? Well, let's just say I could be on one of those public service commercials being all "my life is perfect now that I'm clean".'

Jason laughed, but he had a hunch his friend's life

was far from perfect. He knew Tyler wouldn't have shown up in Malibu without a single change of clothes otherwise. He couldn't help wondering if Tyler was hiding something.

'Holy cow, is that Danielle Who Smells?' Tyler suddenly bellowed. He bolted from the car and rushed toward the house.

'Oh my God!' Jason heard Dani squeal. 'Kristy, gotta go.' She hung up her cell and flung her arms around Tyler. 'Ty the Spy!'

Jason laughed as he headed up the driveway. Dani and Tyler had given each other dumb nicknames when they were all little kids. Tyler picked Dani up and spun her around, and Dani laughed like a maniac. Jason knew Tyler had been her very first crush when she was little. And though she had long grown out of that, she still looked psyched to see him again. He was kind of like a second big brother to her, and Tyler had always treated her like his kid sister.

He's probably missed the whole family since we moved, Jason realized as he watched them. After his parents' divorce, Tyler had spent a lot of time at the Freemans' house. They were more of a family to him than his real one. So it made sense that he'd want to come to them for Thanksgiving. Maybe it was as simple as that, Jason thought, running up to the porch to join Tyler and Dani. Maybe Tyler didn't have anything to hide at all.

Maybe.

FOUR

'Get out of the bathroom!' Dani yelled the next morning. 'Jason!'

Jason pulled open his bedroom door, blinking against the bright morning sunshine, to see his sister waiting near the bathroom at the end of the hallway, yawning. Her hair was in a messy ponytail and she wore her baggy Paul Frank pyjamas with the monkeys on them. 'I'm not in there,' he called to her.

Dani glanced at him and frowned in confusion.

'It must be Tyler,' he said.

Dani's eyes widened in horror and her hand flew to her hair. Without a word, she turned and ran back into her own room, slamming the door behind her. Jason chuckled. His sister was not a morning person – in her tired haze, she'd obviously forgotten Tyler was even there. He figured she'd be perfectly made up, washed and blow-dried by the time she made another appearance.

Tyler stuck his head out of the bathroom door. 'You need to get in here?' he asked Jason.

Jason stared at his friend. The guy looked seriously pale, with deep circles under his eyes. 'Nah, I can wait,' he said. Tyler nodded and disappeared back into the bathroom.

Shaking his head, Jason retreated into his bedroom. Whatever was going on with Tyler, a good night's sleep hadn't solved it. The dude still looked like crap.

But by breakfast time, Tyler seemed to have rebounded. He was busy helping Mrs Freeman mix pancake batter when Jason came into the kitchen.

'. . . and Mr Ruck tripped and knocked over the whole podium,' he was saying.

Jason's mom dissolved into laughter. 'I always hated that guy,' she remarked. 'Ever since we were on the same PTA committee when you and Jason were in third grade.'

'Morning,' Jason said, heading to the fridge for some o.j.

'Happy Thanksgiving,' his mom replied. She grabbed his arm as he passed her and spun him away from the refrigerator. 'We're all sitting down to eat together this morning. I don't want you doing your typical orange juice and banana on the run.'

'She's showing off for Aunt Bianca. I'm even sup-posed to put out the good coffee cups,' Danielle said from the dining room, where she was setting the table. As Jason had expected, she was fully dressed and look-ing perfect.

'I am not showing off,' Mrs Freeman said, handing Jason a basket full of muffins and pointing to the table.

He dutifully carried the muffins over and set them down. 'Yes she is,' he murmured to Dani.

'Totally.' Dani laughed.

'Your Aunt Bianca is here?' Tyler asked from the counter. 'How come I didn't see her last night?'

'She had to go into the office for some last-minute thing,' Mrs Freeman replied. 'She didn't get back until almost midnight.'

'Weird,' Jason said. 'Doesn't everyone try to cut out early the day before Thanksgiving?'

'Not in her job,' Dani put in. 'Dealing with all those high-powered, demanding Hollywood peeps.'

'My ears are burning,' Bianca said, appearing in the kitchen. 'Are you talking about me behind my back?'

'Only good things,' Jason assured her. 'I think Dani wants to have your job after college.'

'Oh, I hope not,' Mrs Freeman said. Aunt Bianca gave her an arch look, and Mrs Freeman shrugged.

'No offense, Bee, but wrangling celebs isn't exactly—'

'Boring?' Dani interrupted. 'I'd love to be a star-creator like Aunt Bianca. With one place in New York and another in California. Traveling all over.' She sat down at the table and grabbed a muffin.

'That's my girl.' Aunt Bianca laughed. 'Be adventurous.'

'Do you have a place out here in California?' Tyler asked, coming to sit next to Dani.

'I don't, actually,' Bianca replied. 'My late husband had a home in Malibu, but I sold it after he died. It made me sad to be there.'

Tyler nodded sympathetically. 'That's tough.'

'Besides, I don't need a place here anymore. I can always stay with my big sis,' Bianca said, grinning at Mrs Freeman. 'And if she gets sick of me, my company will put me up in one of the hotels.'

'I'd take the Beverly Hilton over our house any day,' Dani commented.

'Me, too, if somebody else is paying,' Jason's dad called from the stairway. 'Did I miss breakfast?'

'Nope. The pancakes are ready, so everybody sit,' Mrs Freeman replied.

Jason and his father sat across from Dani and Tyler, and his mom and aunt took the ends. Looking back and forth between them, Jason was surprised at how different the two women were. Somehow he'd never noticed it before. It was more than just their looks, though Bianca's dark hair was nothing like his mother's short blond bob. It was their different attitudes to life that was most striking. His mom was, well, a *mom* – in a good way, of course. But Bianca always acted like she was still just a kid herself. *Well, she is a bit younger than Mom*, Jason thought.

He took a look at Bianca's sweater and jeans ensemble. The outfit would've looked normal on his mother, but on Bianca it seemed uber-stylish. He suddenly remembered what Sienna had said about his aunt and her sense of fashion.

'Hey, Aunt Bianca, do you know Sienna Devereux?' he asked suddenly.

She looked at him in surprise. So did Dani and Tyler.

'Who's Sienna Devereux?' Tyler asked. Dani just widened her eyes in her usual, gossip-detecting way.

'A girl at school,' Jason said, aware of the blush slowly creeping across his cheeks. He cleared his throat. 'My friend Brad's girlfriend.'

'Hmm . . . The name sounds familiar,' Aunt Bianca said. 'Stefan knew the Devereuxs, of course. I probably met her once or twice. Why do you ask?'

'Just wondering,' Jason said. 'She mentioned that she'd met you. Said she likes the way you dress.'

'Oh, well, in that case I love her already,' Bianca joked.

'Jason does too,' Danielle teased. Jason tossed a muffin at her.

'So, Tyler, how long are you staying?' Aunt Bianca asked. 'Do you have to be back for school on Monday?'

Tyler kept his eyes on the pancakes he was smothering with syrup. 'Uh . . . technically. But I can skip a day or two. I'm a senior.'

'When did that become an excuse for cutting class?' Mr Freeman asked.

Tyler finally looked up, and Jason thought he saw a hint of annoyance in his friend's eyes. But it disappeared immediately, and Tyler grinned. 'All I mean is that they're giving SAT practice tests next week, and I already took the SATs, so I don't need to go.'

'Sweet deal,' Jason said. Although when he was at their old school, they certainly hadn't spent days giving SAT practice tests. Had things changed that much?

But as his family continued to chat with his old friend, Jason kept his thoughts to himself. Tyler had always been a favorite with the Freemans. Jason hadn't told his parents about the driving-while-stoned episode from last year. He hadn't told Dani, either.

All that was in the past. Jason planned to leave it there.

'Danielle Who Smells, why aren't you up here playing?' Tyler called a few hours later. 'Jason's too much of a lightweight to be any fun. Look at him all panting and stuff.'

Jason shook his head. They'd only been shooting hoops for fifteen minutes and he wasn't even out of breath. Neither was Tyler, which was a little weird. The guy had looked so exhausted this morning that Jason had figured they were in for a day of sitting in front of the TV while his mom puttered around getting everything ready for the big dinner. But Tyler had obviously got a second wind.

'I'd rather lounge,' Dani answered from her chaise next to the pool. She'd decked herself out in a bikini and a pair of big Jackie O sunglasses. 'Besides, isn't it called one-on-one?'

'Well, yeah, if you're going to get all literal on me,' Tyler grumbled good-naturedly.

Danielle turned back to her book, some chick-lit thing with a drawing of a woman in a leopard-print dress on the front.

'You're just trying to distract me from kicking your ass,' Jason said. 'It won't work.'

'We'll see.' Tyler dribbled the ball toward the hoop mounted on the pool-house wall, ducking and spinning to avoid Jason's coverage. He took a shot – and scored nothing but net. Tyler did a little victory dance, getting in Jason's face.

'I'm still winning, jackass,' Jason pointed out.

Tyler laughed and passed the ball to Jason.

The pool-house door opened, and Bianca came out dressed in a black bathing suit and sandals with little cherries on the toes. 'Time out,' she called. 'I don't want to get hit by any flying basketballs.'

'Wimp,' Jason teased, and she made a face at him as she crossed the court. 'I have to warn you,' he added, lowering his voice, 'that Dani's going to spend the whole day trying to convince you to talk Mom into letting her go to the party.'

'I'm afraid she'll be disappointed, then.' Bianca sighed. 'I've never been able to talk your mother into anything.'

'I can't believe you guys have a pool house,' Tyler commented as Bianca made her way across the grass toward Dani. 'Hell, I can't even believe you have a pool!'

'It's pretty weird,' Jason agreed. 'Almost as weird as being able to sit around in a bathing suit in November.'

Tyler was watching Bianca get herself settled on one of the chaises. 'Dude, your aunt is *hot*,' he said, dropping his voice to a whisper.

Jason rolled his eyes. 'She's my *aunt*, loser,' he replied. 'You can't call her hot in front of me.'

'I'm just saying.' Tyler grinned. 'She's not *my* aunt.'

Jason tossed the ball at him – hard. 'She's, like, forty-two,' he said. 'I think you're a little too young for her.'

'Forty-two?' Tyler repeated. 'Are you serious? She looks amazing.'

Jason glanced over at Bianca. She did look pretty good for her age, now that he thought about it.

'Plastic surgery?' Tyler asked.

'I don't know,' Jason admitted. 'I guess, maybe. People out here seem to think it's normal to get all kinds of lifts and tucks and liposuction. And she does work in Hollywood. It's all about the image.'

'Huh.' Tyler took a lazy shot at the basket and missed. From inside the pool house came a loud crash. 'What was that?' Tyler cried.

'Probably just the pool guy,' Jason said. 'Dad asked him to come by today. He wanted to give him a tip for Thanksgiving.' He crossed over to the pool-house door and pulled it open. Joe, the pool guy, was trying to maneuver the skimmer out of the crowded supplies closet next to the bathroom.

'Need some help?' Jason asked.

'No, I got it,' Joe replied. 'Sorry about the noise, I just knocked over all the vacuum hoses. I'm really out of it today.'

'No problem,' Jason said. 'You don't need to clean the pool on Thanksgiving, though. My dad just wanted to say thanks.'

'I know,' Joe said. 'But I figured while I'm here I might as well skim out the leaves. It'll only take a second.'

'You're a perfectionist,' Jason joked as the guy headed out with the skimmer. He knocked into a palm tree with the long handle and laughed, shaking his head.

'I think he's had a few Turkey Day beers,' Tyler murmured.

Jason chuckled. 'Game on,' he said, grabbing the ball from Tyler. He shot and scored, but Tyler was close behind, immediately making another basket. Jason played harder, really working up a sweat, and for a while the only sounds were from the ball hitting the ground or the wall.

When Danielle and Bianca appeared nearby, Jason jumped. He'd been concentrating so hard that he hadn't even seen them get up from the lounge chairs.

'Mind if we walk through?' Dani asked, nodding toward the pool-house door. 'We need dry towels.'

Tyler held up his hands. 'I need a breather, anyway,' he said.

'What's wrong with your towels?' Jason asked.

Danielle grinned, glanced over her shoulder and lowered her voice. 'Joe dropped the skimmer in the water and totally splashed them,' she said, amused. 'He was so busy staring at Aunt Bianca that he almost fell in the pool himself!'

Bianca nudged her toward the pool house. 'Quiet, he'll hear you! And *you're* the one he was looking at, young lady.'

They disappeared inside, still talking.

'Shouldn't we be helping your mother with dinner?' Tyler asked. 'She's been cooking all day.'

'Go ahead and try to set foot in the kitchen. I dare you,' Jason said. 'It's a Thanksgiving tradition: Mom cooks about twenty different things at once while Dad spends the whole day on the turkey. Every year they almost burn the house down, but they love it.'

'Sounds romantic,' Tyler said flatly.

Jason grimaced. He'd forgotten about the animosity between Tyler's parents. His friend probably didn't want to hear cute stories about happily married couples. 'You want to play anymore?' he asked, trying to change the subject.

'I think I'm done. This sun is too strong.' Tyler pulled off his T-shirt and mopped his sweaty face with it. 'Besides, I'm winning,' he added with a grin.

'No wonder you want to stop,' Jason joked.

Dani pushed open the door and stepped out with a new towel wrapped around her waist. Bianca followed, wearing shorts and a gauzy top. 'I'm going to head inside for a bit,' she said. 'I've got some calls to make for work.' She left them with a little wave.

'Still want that job?' Jason asked his sister. 'Working on Thanksgiving?'

But Dani ignored him. She was staring at Tyler's chest. 'What happened to you?' she asked. 'You're covered in bruises.'

Jason glanced at his friend in surprise. Danielle was right. The entire left side of Tyler's rib cage was covered in the sickly yellowish marks of bruises that were starting to heal.

'Oh. It's . . . uh . . . it's nothing.' Tyler replied, quickly pulling his T-shirt back on to cover the bruising.

'Did you get mugged or something while you were hitching here?' Jason asked, thinking that it would explain Tyler's lack of clothes and belongings.

'Are you kidding?' Tyler put on one of his patented mega-watt grins. 'Who would mug someone as sweet as me?' He jumped up and grabbed the ball, passing it to Jason energetically. 'Let's go, man, game on!'

He's trying to distract us from the bruises, Jason thought. *What is up with him?* 'I thought you were done,' he said aloud.

'I have a few more spectacular shots in me,' Tyler replied. 'Unless I've hurt your pride too much already.'

'No more hoops,' Mrs Freeman called from the French doors that led into the living room. 'Dinner's in an hour. Everyone get ready.'

'Get ready?' Tyler repeated. 'Is this a dress-up thing?' He took a dubious sniff at his sweat-covered T-shirt.

'I don't know about dress-up, but it's definitely not a smelly T-shirt affair,' Danielle replied, laughing.

Tyler looked dismayed, and Jason grinned. 'Don't worry, I can spot you some threads.'

'Thanks.' Tyler followed Jason into the house. 'We never do the whole big Thanksgiving thing. My dad's version of giving thanks is eating turkey in front of the tube so he doesn't miss any football games.'

'How is your dad?' Jason asked tentatively. After the divorce, Tyler hadn't wanted to talk about his parents at all. Maybe he was starting to deal with it a little now.

'Who knows? I barely see the guy,' Tyler replied. 'I spend as little time at home as I can. I can't wait for graduation so I can get out of there.'

Jason didn't know what to say. It seemed like things for Tyler were worse at home than they'd ever been. He noticed Danielle shooting Tyler a sympathetic look as they climbed the stairs to the second floor. He never understood why, but girls seemed to like troubled guys.

'I'm thinking green and orange striped polo shirt for you,' he said, 'with maybe a pair of plaid golf pants.'

'You wish,' Tyler replied, seeming relieved at the change of subject.

'Hey, you have no clothes. You're at my mercy,' Jason warned. When they reached the upstairs hallway, he turned toward his bedroom. 'Let me just grab some stuff.'

Tyler and Dani headed down the hall toward their rooms while Jason pulled a pair of khakis and a blue button-down shirt from his closet. He snagged a pair of jeans and a few T-shirts, too. If Tyler was going to be here all weekend, he'd need more than just one change of clothes. He took them down to the guest room where Tyler was staying.

The door was open, so Jason went in. Tyler was over by the window, cell phone to his ear. Probably listening to a voicemail message, Jason figured. He dumped the clothes on the bed and turned to leave. His sneaker tangled in Tyler's hoodie, which was lying on the floor near the foot of the bed, and Jason nearly tripped up. He bent to pick up the sweatshirt and a prescription pill bottle tumbled out of the pocket, so he swooped back down to grab that, too. 'Sorry, man,' he said, tossing the hoodie on top of the other clothes on the bed.

He reached out to put the pills on the dresser so they wouldn't get lost. But as Jason glanced down at the bottle in his hand, he hesitated. Something was wrong.

The name on the label wasn't Tyler's.

FIVE

'What are you doing?' Tyler snapped, his voice tense.

Jason turned to find his friend off the phone. 'Sorry,' he said again. 'I fell over your hoodie and almost kicked your pills across the room.' He tossed the bottle to Tyler. 'I didn't want you to lose them.'

'Thanks.' Tyler quickly shoved the bottle into the pocket of his jeans.

'What are they for?' Jason asked. 'You sick?'

'No, they're just, uh, painkillers,' Tyler replied, frowning.

'For the bruises?' Jason pushed. He knew Tyler didn't appreciate the questions, but he wasn't about to back down. His friend was walking around with someone else's pills, hitching across the country with no supplies, and covered in bruises. He'd have to be blind or stupid not to have noticed something was wrong.

'Yeah.' Tyler clearly wasn't intending to say anymore, but Jason held his gaze until finally Tyler sighed. 'I got banged up a week or so ago and the doctor gave me some pills for the pain.'

'Banged up how?' Jason asked.

'Playing football,' Tyler said. 'You know how it is.'

'Not really,' Jason replied. 'I don't play football. Neither do you.'

Tyler just stared at him for a moment, and Jason knew he'd busted the guy. Tyler was a swimmer, not a football player. It was one of the things they had in common – both liked watching a good game on the weekend, but neither one of them liked to play. 'Yeah, well, that's why I got banged up,' Tyler said at last. 'I suck.' He smiled nervously, clearly wondering whether Jason would buy it.

Jason frowned. He knew Tyler was lying about the bruises, and lying about the pills being prescribed for him. The question was, why? He'd come all the way to Malibu to see Jason – why not tell him the truth? 'Look, Ty—' Jason began.

'Do you seriously have a shirt from Disneyland?' Tyler interrupted, grabbing one of the T-shirts from the bed. 'What are you, five years old?'

Jason stifled a sigh. Clearly, Tyler was determined not to talk about anything serious. But then, maybe that was just what he needed: a break – a vacation from whatever was going on in his life back home. It kind of worried Jason that his friend was taking medication that had been prescribed for somebody else. But he felt that it wasn't any of his business – unless Tyler wanted it to be. And right now, it was obvious that he didn't.

'They were giving them out for free at an Angels game,' Jason explained. 'Besides, that shirt would be pretty big on a five year old.'

Tyler chuckled. 'Thanks for the loan. Guess I better shower before dinner, huh?'

'Good luck getting in there before Dani!' Jason laughed, heading for the door. 'See you downstairs.'

'Everything looks amazing, Mrs F,' Tyler said as they all sat down around the dining-room table. Jason had to agree. His mom had made the place look like a TV special on the perfect Thanksgiving holiday.

The table was decked out with all the new linens and china Jason's mother had bought when they moved to California. It had less of a wintry feel than their dining room in Michigan had. Here everything was a shade of light green or blue and felt summery. Even the candles in the middle of the table were blue and smelled like the ocean.

'Thank you, Tyler,' Mrs Freeman said. 'I only hope the food lives up to it.'

'Don't pretend to be all modest,' Aunt Bianca told her sister with a smile. 'You know you're a great cook.'

'I'm sure it's not up to your standards,' Mrs Freeman replied. She turned to Tyler. 'My little sister only eats in the best restaurants in New York and L.A.'

Bianca rolled her eyes. 'I just don't see the point in cooking myself when other people do it so much better.'

Jason knew his mom and his aunt always bickered to some degree, but the sisters seemed to be getting on each other's nerves a little more than usual during this visit. Jason glanced at Dani, and she shrugged.

'Here's the main event,' Mr Freeman said, coming in from the kitchen with the turkey on a platter. He placed it down in the center of the table. 'Should I carve now or wait until everyone's had their salad?'

'No salad for me,' Jason said. 'I like to get right to the meat.'

'Me too,' Tyler seconded.

Jason's dad nodded. 'OK, I'll carve now.'

'Why don't we let Jason carve?' Bianca suggested. 'He's a big, strapping man now. Let him take over the carving duties.'

Dani almost spit out her mouthful of water, and Tyler laughed out loud.

'A big, strapping man? Freeman?' he teased.

Even Jason had to laugh. 'That's OK, Aunt Bianca. I don't need to carve a turkey to feel like a man,' he said reassuringly.

But Jason noticed that Bianca actually looked a little put out at having her suggestion dismissed so lightly. Maybe that was why, with a slight tone of irritation, she said, 'I just think it's time we stopped treating you like a child. You're almost done with school. Soon you'll have to start making your own decisions.'

'Well, that's true. I guess you're right and I'd better get some practice in by carving the turkey,' Jason said with a smile. He knew Tyler and Danielle would make fun of him for the rest of the weekend, but he was anxious to calm things down and lighten the atmosphere. He stood up, took the carving knife from his dad, and got to work.

Aunt Bianca shook her head. 'Can you believe how grown up he is?' she asked Jason's parents. 'Dani too. In a few years they'll be off at college.'

'Off at college,' Dani repeated, nodding. 'College – where there are lots of parties!'

Mrs Freeman sighed. 'Danielle—' she began.

'Mom,' Dani interrupted. 'Your guru, Dr Phil, would

say to let me go to Zach's. He'd say that I need experience dealing with parties while I'm still in the safety of my home, with my big brother to look after me.'

Jason choked back a laugh. So Dani had resorted to invoking Dr Phil! Well, it just might work.

'Dr Phil doesn't have all the facts in this case,' Mrs Freeman answered.

'What facts does he need that—?' Danielle began.

'End of discussion,' Jason's mom said firmly.

'I'm getting flashes of us and Mom,' Bianca commented lightly to her sister. 'Remember how overprotective she always was? Remember how we used to have to sneak out and—?'

'Looking back, I think she might have been right,' Jason's mother said, cutting Bianca off sharply. Then her voice softened. 'Maybe it's something you don't realize until you're a parent yourself. It wouldn't have hurt the two of us to listen to Mom a little more back then.' She grinned. 'Not that I'll tell her that any time soon. I don't want to face an attack of the I-told-you-sos.'

'You know, Stefan was friends with the Lafrenières for years,' Bianca put in soothingly. 'I'm sure you don't have to worry about Dani at their son's party.' Jason figured Bianca was just trying to help Dani out, but he knew she had just pushed his mother a little too far.

'That's it,' Mrs Freeman snapped. 'Danielle, I told you – no. Bee, this is none of your business!'

Jason glanced at Tyler. His friend looked seriously uncomfortable. The last thing he needed was a family feud at dinner – he'd had enough of that in his own house. Jason hoped Bianca would just let the party thing drop.

'You want Danielle to make friends with the right people, don't you?' Aunt Bianca pressed. 'Well, the Lafrenières do more charity work than anyone else in Malibu! There are some valuable contacts to be made. You have to want that for Dani and Jason.'

'Don't tell me what I "have to want",' Mrs Freeman said, her voice rising. 'The answer is no. Those parties are too wild, and Danielle is not going.'

Nobody spoke for a moment, and Jason was afraid that the day would be completely ruined. There was a weird energy in the air, and he didn't know where it was coming from. But everyone was on edge.

Bianca opened her mouth to say something else, but Danielle jumped in. 'Don't worry. I'll just go to the movies or something on Friday,' she volunteered quickly, her eyes darting between her mother and Bianca. Jason could see that she was clearly wishing she'd never brought the party up at all. 'It's no biggie.

It's not like being refused the last scoop of mashed potatoes. They look great, by the way, Mom.'

'Everything's great, Tania,' Jason's dad agreed. 'Let's enjoy it. It's Thanksgiving.'

That was enough for Bianca to think better of whatever she'd been about to say. She nodded and fell silent.

'Well I for one have a lot to be thankful for this Thanksgiving,' Tyler said, raising his glass of apple cider. 'And I'd like to propose a toast to all of you, the Freemans. Thank you for including me in your Thanksgiving. You've always made me feel right at home, and today is no exception.'

Jason's mom smiled and Aunt Bianca chuckled. 'You mean because we're willing to argue in front of you just like you're part of the family?'

'Exactly,' Tyler said with a grin. Everybody laughed, relaxing for the first time since they'd taken their seats.

Jason shot his friend a grateful look. Tyler had always been able to charm anyone – from senior citizens to toddlers. This time he may have saved Thanksgiving.

'OK, pass your plates for turkey,' Jason announced. 'And let's eat!'

'Sorry I mentioned the P word at dinner,' Dani said later that night. She, Jason, and Tyler were heading upstairs for bed after they'd finished cleaning up the kitchen. 'I didn't know it would set things off like that.'

'You always used to go to parties back in Michigan,' Tyler said. 'What's the difference?'

'The parties are more out of control here. But I'll deny saying it if you try to quote me. Mom's parent-noid enough as it is,' Dani answered, pulling her cell phone out of the pocket of her trendy shrunken blazer. She changed the faceplate every day, and today her cell was zebra-striped. 'I'm going to call Billy. He's the only one I know who isn't going to Zach's. He'll come up with something fun for Friday night.'

'Ooh, Billy,' Tyler teased. 'That your boyfriend?'

Dani rolled her eyes. 'I still haven't picked out the lucky guy who gets to be my *boyfriend*,' she answered. 'But it definitely won't be Billy, because he's gay.' She hit a speed-dial number on her cell. 'What's shakin', Billy?' she asked, wandering toward her room.

'See you in the morning,' Jason told Tyler. 'Thanks for putting up with my family.'

'You kidding? Your family should get an award for Most Functional Thanksgiving. Nobody even got close to throwing food or crying.'

Jason laughed. 'True. Although I think my mom might've lobbed the gravy at Aunt Bianca if she hadn't spent so much time making it.' He slapped Tyler's hand and headed down the hall to his bedroom. The basketball combined with the huge dinner had made him sleepy, and he flung himself down on the bed fully dressed. He'd rest for a few minutes, wait for Dani and Tyler to use the bathroom, then go brush his teeth.

But he'd only been lying there for a minute or two when a noise at the window startled him. It was a soft bang, followed by silence, then another little bang. Almost like someone was tapping from outside. Jason got up and went over to peer out.

The moon was almost full, and it cast an eerie silver light over the backyard, reflecting up from the still surface of the pool. The carefully spaced potted trees around the back deck threw distorted shadows onto the ground. As Jason watched, one of them moved.

He leaned closer to the window, staring into the darkness as someone stepped out into the moonlight.

Silver light on sleek black hair. Pale, perfect skin, luminescent in the darkness. *Sienna.*

Jason threw open the window and leaned out.

'Hey, Michigan,' Sienna called quietly. 'Can I come up?'

Sienna was at his house, asking to climb up to his room. Jason felt as if he had died and gone to heaven.

Yeah, he thought. *If heaven's like an episode of* Dawson's Creek*!* He glanced at the vine-covered trellis that rose from the back deck up to the top of the house. It ran about a foot to the left of his window and it would be pretty easy to climb now that he thought about it. 'Sure. Come on up. As long as you don't call me Dawson,' he told Sienna.

She just gave him that slow, sly smile of hers, then put one slim hand on the bottom of the trellis and gracefully pulled herself up, shimmying her way toward him as if she'd done it a million times. Before Jason knew it, she was level with his window.

'Want to give me a hand?' she asked, her voice husky.

Jason put his hands on her waist to steady her as she edged sideways and slid one long leg over his windowsill. Then the other leg.

'What are you doing here?' he asked, forcing himself to let go of her. 'Not that I'm not pleased to see you.'

'I need to talk to you.' She raised one eyebrow. 'But, er, is your cell turned off this time?'

Her question brought him right back to that moment in the car. When they'd been about to kiss. Sienna moved closer. Almost as close as she'd been that day.

'I threw the thing away,' Jason joked. He waited for Sienna to start talking; instead, she reached out and cupped his face in her hands, her body leaning into his.

Jason's brain was trying to tell him something – something about Brad, about vampires, about Sienna being off-limits. But his body overpowered it. He had to kiss her. Now. He leaned in, wrapping his arms around her.

Sienna tilted his head to one side and sunk her teeth into his neck. Electric pain shot through Jason as he felt her begin to feed. He pushed her away, forced to use all his strength.

Sienna stumbled backwards. Her dark eyes had turned yellowish and they gleamed with desire. But not desire for Jason, just for his blood. And he'd seen that look before – in the eyes of Luke Archer.

Sienna laughed as she reached for Jason again. Her fangs gleamed white and sharp in the moonlight and her gaze was focused on his throat. There was no sign of the girl he knew within those animal eyes. There was only the bloodlust.

And Jason knew she was about to drink from him until he was dead.

SIX

'Get away from me!' Jason yelled, pushing Sienna away with all his strength. She fell to the floor. And he sat up. In bed. Alone.

He stared around the room, but there was no one there. The window was closed. 'It was a dream,' he muttered, in relief. He'd obviously fallen asleep waiting for the bathroom. Breathing hard – whether from fear or excitement he wasn't sure – Jason got up and yanked open the door. The hallway was empty.

He stalked down to the bathroom and splashed his face with cold water. *Of course it was a dream,* he thought, beginning to decelerate. *Sienna would never come here, never come on to me like that. I've clearly absorbed too many of those* Dawson's Creek *reruns Dani's always watching.* But it had seemed so real. The feel of her in his arms.

And the look of bloodlust in her eyes.

Jason shoved the thought away and focused on getting

ready for bed. But once back in his room in the dark, he couldn't shake the thoughts of Sienna. What the hell was with that dream? He knew Sienna would never feed on him. He knew she'd never give in to the bloodlust. She'd told him that it was forbidden, and he believed her.

It's because of today, he thought. *There was some kind of strange energy at dinner and it must've got into my head and into my dreams.*

He pounded his pillow into a ball and tried to get to sleep. But thoughts of Sienna kept playing on his mind, keeping him awake until well after two in the morning. At last, finally, he drifted off.

This time, he didn't dream at all.

On Friday morning, Jason was the last one downstairs. Bianca was reading the paper at the dining-room table. Dani sat yawning at the breakfast bar, and Tyler was shoveling cereal into his mouth.

'Where's Mom?' Jason asked, surprised to find his father manning the coffee machine.

'Gone already,' Mr Freeman replied. 'She took the leftovers over to the town hall. They're doing a donated food run to a homeless shelter.'

'Cool,' Jason said. He grabbed a bowl and sat next to Tyler for some cereal.

'I'm going to head into L.A. this morning for a little retail therapy,' Aunt Bianca said from the dining room. 'Want to come, Dani?'

Danielle's eyes lit up at the prospect of shopping. 'Definitely!' Then she glanced at Jason. 'What are you guys doing today?'

'Adam and I promised to show Tyler the beach,' he said.

'Maybe I'll stop by after,' Danielle decided. She finished her juice. 'Surfrider Beach?'

Jason nodded. 'Yep. Best waves around.'

'Can't come to Malibu without checking out the waves,' Tyler added. But he didn't sound that enthused.

Bianca stood up and stretched. 'Ready?' she asked Danielle.

'You don't even have to ask,' Dani answered, grinning as they headed out.

Jason finished his cereal. 'Ready?' he asked Tyler as he stuck his bowl in the sink.

'You don't even have to ask,' Tyler replied, but it was a weak-ass imitation of Dani. His voice was way too calm and flat, and Jason noticed that the circles under his friend's eyes were even deeper and darker than they had been yesterday.

Jason walked out to the front hall and grabbed his

surfboard. 'We can take turns. Or we can rent you a board.'

'Whatever,' Tyler said as he followed Jason to the car. He got in, settled back in the seat and didn't say a word until they arrived at the beach. Jason wondered what was going on with his friend. He'd never seen Tyler so moody before, not even right after his parents' break-up.

'I'm going to hit the bathroom,' Tyler said as soon as Jason parked.

Jason got out of the car and stared down at the beach. It was a calm day, and the water was practically still. It looked more like the Henderson Marina back in Michigan than the Pacific Ocean. He figured that the mood Tyler was in, he probably wouldn't care, but the flat water tortured Jason. He wanted his board time.

But then he noticed something else to torture him: Sienna. Well, Sienna and Brad, with Belle Rémy, her boyfriend Dominic, Zach, and a few other kids from the Heights. A few other *vampires*. Jason's mind instantly flew to the dream he'd had last night – the dream that had kept him tossing and turning for hours. Sienna so close. That kiss about to happen.

How was he going to just walk over there and say hello to her as if he hadn't been thinking about her for the past ten hours?

'Let's go, bro!' Tyler boomed, jogging over from the bathroom. He smacked Jason on the back. 'Show me those California sands!'

Jason stared at him. The bags under his eyes were still there, but otherwise Tyler was like a whole different guy. He grabbed the cooler from the backseat and rushed down the wooden steps from the parking lot to the beach. Jason grabbed his board – just in case the waves got going later – and raced after him.

'Freeman!' Brad called, waving. 'Over here!'

'Friends of yours?' Tyler teased as they headed over.

'Nah. I'm just kind of a celebrity around Malibu,' Jason said. 'The guy on the white towel is Zach. The one giving the party.'

'The most popular guy on the face of the planet!' Tyler exclaimed, doing a much better Danielle impersonation than he had in the kitchen.

'And very, very rich,' Jason added.

'Lucky bastard,' Tyler joked.

'Hey, Jason.' Belle ambled over to meet them, her long, athletic legs moving easily over the sand. 'Who's your friend?'

Jason shot a look at Dominic, who was glaring at them from his seat on a dark blue beach blanket. He existed in a constant state of insane jealousy, and Belle seemed to like to get him all tweaked. She was already giving Tyler one of her best flirty smiles.

'Tyler Deegan, Belle Rémy,' Jason said quickly. 'And her boyfriend,' he added with a nod toward Dominic.

'Hey,' Tyler said. Jason could tell he got the hint when he raised his voice and called to Dominic. 'Hey, man.'

Belle backed off, pouting a little, and Dominic slowly relaxed enough to nod hello.

'Come sit with us,' Brad called, waving them over to a red and white striped blanket set up under a huge white umbrella. An open cooler sat in its shade, bottles of water, beer, and soda spilling over the top along with the ice. Sienna lounged in the sun just next to it. As Jason approached, she sat up and pulled her sunglasses down to look at him.

'Hi,' she said in the same husky voice she'd had in his dream. Jason's throat went dry. He had a bad feeling he was about to make a complete ass of himself.

He was right: the PowerPuff Girl theme rang out from his pocket: 'Dani, I'm going to massacre you,' he muttered. But he was glad to have a reason to turn away from Sienna as he pulled out his cell phone. 'Hello?'

'Jason, it's Adam. Help me out here,' said his friend's voice.

'What's up?' Jason asked.

'I'm in the parking lot. I see your Bug. But where are you?'

'Adam, have you even come down to the beach yet?' Jason asked.

'No,' Adam replied. 'Why?'

'Because if you bothered to look, you'd see me about twenty yards from the stairs,' Jason told him.

'Yeah, but that requires effort,' Adam pointed out. 'This way I don't even have to look.'

'Just for that I'm not going to tell you if we're to the left or the right,' Jason said. He hung up as Adam appeared at the top of the steps. He gave a wave and bounced down the stairs, kicking off his shoes at the bottom. Then he made a big show of hopping barefoot across the hot beach.

'Oh, take it like a man,' Jason called.

Adam grimaced. 'That is some hot sand,' he protested, flinging himself onto the blanket next to Sienna, grabbing some ice from the cooler, and rubbing it on his feet.

'That's disgusting,' Sienna said, but she shook her head in amusement.

Jason had to hand it to the guy – Adam had managed to make himself right at home on Sienna's blanket. Maybe that was because he didn't have any confusing hot-and-freaky dreams to contend with.

'Jason's being rude,' Sienna said, glancing up at Tyler. 'I heard him introduce you to Belle. I'm Sienna.'

'Sienna, huh?' Tyler replied. 'I've heard about you.'

Her eyes immediately went to Jason, and he wanted to smack his old friend in the head.

'What did he tell you?' Sienna asked, immediately turning back to Tyler.

'Lots of mysterious things.' Tyler sat right down on the blanket next to her and leaned in as if he was about to tell her a secret.

Zach gave Jason his usual cool nod as Jason sank down on the blanket between him and Tyler. Jason had known Zach long enough to know that he wasn't the most friendly guy ever born. He was always polite, but never especially enthusiastic. Of all the vampires Jason had met, Zach was the one who most liked to keep to himself.

Jason leaned across Tyler toward Sienna. 'My friend has only recently been released from a . . . let's call it a mental-health facility,' he told her in a loud whisper. 'Compulsive lying is a side effect of his treatment.'

Sienna gave him a light push and turned her attention back to Tyler. 'So, think any of what you heard about me is true?'

'You'll have to tell me,' Tyler murmured, ignoring Jason.

'OK. So what are these mysterious things you've heard?' Sienna asked, and even Adam leaned in to listen.

'Well . . .' Tyler said, drawing it out as long as he could. 'Apparently, you like the way Jason's aunt dresses.'

Sienna's eyebrows shot up. 'Wow, that *is* mysterious,' she laughed. 'What else?'

'That's pretty much it, actually,' Tyler said, lying back on the blanket.

Adam and Sienna laughed.

She looked up at Jason. 'You suck at gossip,' she informed him.

'Well, what can I say? I don't like to talk behind people's backs,' Jason replied virtuously, struggling to keep a straight face.

'Not true. I've heard you describe our history teacher as a hottie on more than one occasion,' Adam put in. 'He likes the way Ms Buchanan's butt looks when she reaches up to write at the top of the blackboard,' he added to Sienna and Tyler.

'Oh, really?' Sienna asked laughingly.

'Hey, Buchanan's got back. Can I help it if I notice?'

Jason grabbed a beer, trying to cover his embarrassment. He knew they were just teasing him, but somehow it was always worse when Sienna was involved.

'So you can give us all the dirt on Freeman, huh?' Brad asked Tyler, admirably un-phased by the fact that Tyler was practically sitting in Sienna's lap.

'Whatever you want to know,' Tyler replied.

'Who was his first love?' Sienna asked immediately.

'Wait!' Adam cried. He rummaged in his backpack and pulled out his mini-camcorder. 'This I have to get on camera.'

'Tyler, don't you want to hit the water?' Jason asked.

'Are you kidding?' Sienna said. 'I'm not letting go of him until I hear all your secrets.'

Tyler shot Jason a mischievous look, then leaned in and whispered in Sienna's ear.

'Hey, share it with the rest of the class!' Adam complained.

'Sorry,' Tyler said to Adam, drawing back from Sienna, but only a little. 'Jason's first love, I'm sorry to say, broke his heart.'

'Compulsive liar, see,' Jason reminded Sienna, under the feeble cover of a loud cough.

Adam spun to focus the camera on Jason's face.

Jason reached out and plucked it from his hand, turning it off.

'Broke his heart how?' Sienna asked.

'She left him for another guy,' Tyler explained sorrowfully. 'Unfortunately for Jason, he just couldn't compete with me.'

'You?' Sienna cried.

'You hit on your friend's girlfriend?' Zach asked.

Jason was surprised to hear him join the conversation. His tone was casual, but Jason found it interesting that Zach cared enough to ask. He couldn't help wondering if Zach had somehow picked up on his feelings for Sienna.

'Nah, she hit on me,' Tyler said. 'That happens a lot, you know?'

'Right, because you're irresistible,' Sienna said, trying to look serious.

'I'm glad you noticed,' Tyler replied.

Jason shook his head. *Yeah*, he thought, laughing. *Tyler can charm anyone.*

'So she hit on you and you went out with her?' Sienna was saying, her gaze focused on Tyler even though Brad's arm was around her. 'You bad boy!'

'I was only eight years old,' Tyler replied with a wink. 'All I did was sit with her at lunch one day.'

Sienna and Brad laughed, and Sienna turned to Jason. 'Did you forgive him?'

'I made him give me his top three baseball cards and lend me his GameBoy first. Then I forgave him,' Jason said.

'Fascinating though this is,' Adam put in, 'I'd rather hear about the more recent adventures of our boy hero. Don't you have any good Freeman-in-high-school stories?'

'Sure,' Tyler said. 'Which do you want to hear first, the time Jason stole a keg from a 7-11, or the time he had three different dates to the same dance?'

Sienna was still holding Jason's gaze. 'The one with the dates,' she said. 'Absolutely.'

'I don't need to hear this. I was there. I lived it,' Jason said. He stood up and grabbed his board. 'Besides, I need to get some practice in before my next lesson with the Surf Rabbi.'

'Those waves look about your speed,' Adam joked, gazing out at the ocean which remained as smooth as glass.

'It's all about feeling the water with your soul, heathen,' Jason answered. Then he ran toward the surf. The baby waves wouldn't be much of a challenge, but he had a feeling that watching Sienna as she listened to a rundown of his love life might be.

Except that the very fact she wanted to hear about said love life showed that she had some interest in him. *An interesting kind of interest,* Jason thought, grinning to himself as he splashed into the water.

When he returned to the flotilla of blankets, Dani had joined the group.

Jason dropped down on the blanket next to her. 'Not going in the water?' he asked.

'Maybe later,' she replied, yawning. 'I think I'm going to nap first. I got no sleep last night.'

'Why?' Jason asked. He was damn sure Danielle hadn't been awake for the same reason he had!

'Tyler was on the phone all night,' Dani said, keeping her voice low. 'The wall between our rooms is so thin. Every time I went to sleep, his stupid cell would ring and wake me up again. He probably kept losing the signal like we do. He was talking really loud whenever he was on.'

'Who was he talking to?' Jason asked.

'How should I know?' Dani said. 'But he got at least four calls, and it sounded kind of serious. I heard him say he needed more time. He kept saying that two days wasn't enough.'

'Enough for what?'

'I don't know.' Dani bit her lip. 'He's been acting weird ever since he got here.'

'So you noticed too,' Jason said.

'Of course I noticed. It's totally not like him,' Dani said. 'Tyler's usually so funny and laid-back – which he still has been some of the time – but the rest . . .' She shook her head. 'I don't know. He's been kind of hyper.'

Jason didn't answer. He knew Tyler had been acting differently since before they left Michigan, but Dani didn't know that. And he didn't want to tell her. Her crush was long gone, but she still had a major soft spot for his old friend. Why ruin that?

'He sounded pretty upset last night,' Danielle said thoughtfully. 'I think he may be in some kind of trouble. I'm a little worried about him.' She stretched out on the blanket and closed her eyes.

Jason also lay back. He wanted to catch up on his sleep. But, though he was tired, his mind refused to switch off and let him relax. Tyler had him more than a little worried, too . . .

SEVEN

Was Tyler in trouble? Jason didn't know what to think. What were the mysterious, middle-of-the-night phone calls about? Why would Tyler need more time? Jason had assumed Tyler's moodiness was because of his less than stellar home life. But maybe there was more to it.

Jason figured he would try to find some time to sound Tyler out about his situation later. Now wasn't the time – there were too many people around. Eventually, he drifted off to sleep.

By the time he woke up, the sun had moved halfway across the sky. Somebody had repositioned the umbrella to cover him, and the entire group was gone. Jason sat up groggily and looked around. He spotted Tyler in the water with Brad and Dominic, Adam filming them from the shore. Belle stood with the surf breaking over her toes, watching.

Danielle was swimming nearby. Her friends Kristy and Billy had shown up.

'I think you were drooling,' said a voice from behind him.

Jason quickly wiped his mouth, then turned to find Sienna laughing. 'You've caught the lying thing from Ty,' he accused with a smile.

'You're definitely more gullible than I expected,' she replied. 'Have a nice nap?'

He stretched his arms above his head, working out the stiffness that came from lying on the sand. 'I didn't get much sleep last night,' he explained.

'How come?'

Because I was thinking about you, he thought. 'I don't know. Too much food, maybe,' he said aloud, hoping his voice sounded casual.

Sienna looked at him silently for a long moment, and Jason felt a sudden pang of nerves. It was almost as if she knew what he was thinking. Or else maybe she wanted to talk about the fact that they'd come close to kissing the other day. The air between them felt thick with energy. He wasn't sure if he moved toward her or she moved toward him, but suddenly they were only a foot apart on the blanket, and her long bare leg was touching his.

'Sienna! Come help me,' Brad called from the water.

She turned away, and Jason felt cold.

Brad stood up, shaking droplets of water from his hair. 'Can you bring me my goggles?' he called to Sienna. 'I got salt in my eyes.'

Sienna rummaged around in Brad's bag. As she stood up with the swim goggles, she reached out and ran her fingers through Jason's hair. He shaded his eyes and looked up at her.

'Your hair's a mess from sleeping,' she said quickly. Then she was gone.

Danielle and Tyler passed her on their way back up from the water. Tyler bent over and shook his long hair over Jason, purposely flinging water on him.

'Loser,' Jason commented.

'Sweet life you have here,' Tyler said, dropping down onto the blanket. 'The ocean is great!'

'Does it make you miss the swim team?' Jason asked, figuring that the question didn't sound too leading, but might give him some info about what was going on with Tyler.

Tyler gazed out at the horizon. 'If the school pool had a view like this, it would.'

Dani pulled her wallet from her big straw bag. 'Adam and I are going to go get some bubble tea,' she told Jason. 'You want?'

'What the hell is bubble tea?' Tyler asked.

'It's this disgusting Taiwanese iced tea with big round globs of tapioca in it,' Jason told him. 'The tea is fine, but when you suck up a tapioca ball, it's like ingesting a loogie.'

'Oh, gross,' Dani cried. 'You are such a Neanderthal. It's delicious.'

'I think I'll pass,' Tyler said.

'Suit yourselves.' Dani walked off across the sand toward the snack bar a quarter of a mile away. Adam jogged over to join her. That left Jason and Tyler on the beach.

'Only in Malibu does the snack bar serve Taiwanese bubble tea and lobster rolls instead of Coke and hot dogs,' Jason said. 'Crazy place.'

'I could get used to it,' Tyler replied.

'Too bad you have to leave so soon.' Jason searched his friend's face. 'When do you have to be back in Michigan?'

Tyler shrugged, still gazing at the ocean. 'Whenever.'

'Oh.' Jason hesitated, then plunged ahead. 'Because Dani heard you saying you only had two days.'

'What?' Tyler asked, his attention snapping back to Jason.

'She heard you on your cell last night, I guess. She said it rang several times.' Jason tried to make his voice sound casual.

Tyler grimaced. 'Sorry. I hope I didn't keep her up.'

'I think you did a bit,' Jason replied. 'And she was a little worried about you. She said you kept saying you needed more time. Who were you on the phone with?'

'Just, er, you know . . . my girlfriend.' Tyler sighed. 'She's the needy type. She didn't even want me to come out here, and now she wants me to get back to Michigan as soon as I can.'

'Your girlfriend?' Jason repeated. 'Who? I didn't even know you were seeing anyone.'

'Yeah. You don't know her,' Tyler said vaguely. 'I'm really sorry if I bothered your sister.'

Jason wasn't sure what to say. Dani had made it sound as if there was something sinister about the phone calls, and Tyler's explanation didn't really add up. But it wasn't any of Jason's business who the guy talked to on his phone, or when.

Besides, surely if Tyler was in some kind of trouble, he'd tell me about it, Jason thought. *Wouldn't he? Especially since I've given him so many openings.*

'Later, my friends. We're taking off,' Brad said, as he, Sienna and Zach approached the blankets.

Jason glanced at Sienna. Her hair was wet from swimming and droplets of water slid down her smooth, tanned skin. She was hot when she was fully dressed and dry. Right now, she was scorching. Jason didn't want to get caught staring at her with his tongue dragging in the sand, so he dragged his eyes away.

'You're all leaving?' Tyler asked.

'We've been here for hours,' Belle replied. She gathered up her stuff while Dominic shook out the blanket. 'And we have to get ready for the party tonight.'

'Translation: Sienna and Belle have to spend the next five hours doing their hair,' Brad joked. He took down the umbrella and folded it up.

'And I have to spend the next five hours party-proofing the house,' Zach put in. 'My father's afraid we'll trash the place.'

'See you guys at the party,' Sienna said. She'd wrapped a sarong around her waist, and it clung to her hips as she picked up her beach bag.

'I don't know,' Tyler said. 'I haven't been invited to this infamous party.'

'Infamous?' Zach queried.

Jason rolled his eyes. 'Danielle is pissed because my mom won't let her go. They've been fighting about it all week.'

'Why can't she go?' Zach asked, frowning. 'She's always welcome.'

'My mom freaked out about Carrie Smith, and I

don't blame her,' Jason said evenly. He knew Zach would understand what he really meant – that maybe a vampire-filled house wasn't where he wanted his sister to be.

Zach thought about that, then nodded.

'But you should come, Ty,' Brad put in. 'Mrs Freeman can't tell *you* no.'

Tyler shrugged. 'That's up to Jason.'

'Well, of course *Jason* wants you to come,' Belle said. 'Don't you, Jason?'

Jason hesitated. The last time they were at a party together, Tyler had got stoned and driven off in Jason's car. *Nah, won't happen again*, Jason told himself. *Tyler said all that garbage was behind him.*

'Sure, Tyler and I will both be there,' Jason said aloud. He just hoped he wouldn't regret it.

'Maybe just a movie,' Dani was saying as Jason pulled the VW into the driveway of the house later. She'd been on her cell ever since they left the beach. 'Hello? Billy?' she said, raising her voice. Frustrated, she hit 'End'. 'I lost the signal,' she complained.

'Why didn't you make plans with him while we were at the beach?' Jason asked. He found it baffling how much time she spent on the phone with her friends.

She'd called Billy about three minutes after saying goodbye to him at Surfrider Beach.

Danielle ignored him, shoving open her car door and climbing out. Tyler swung himself over the side of the convertible without bothering to use the door.

'It's a little cramped in the back, bro,' Tyler joked. 'Not enough room for me and all the beach gear.'

'When I get a car, it'll be bigger,' Dani said. She pulled the wet towels out of the back seat and shoved them into Tyler's arms, then grabbed her straw bag. 'Straight to the laundry room,' she told Tyler. 'Mom hates when we leave towels around.'

'Got it.' Tyler took off toward the house, Dani following.

Jason dragged the blanket out of the back and shook it out one more time. If their mom hated wet towels, she *really* hated sand in the house. As he started toward the front door, a cell phone chirped from the car. He turned around and scanned the VW, finally spotting Dani's phone – gray faceplate today – on the front seat. Jason figured it was probably Billy calling back.

He grabbed it, hit 'Talk' and said, 'Hello?'

'Time is running out,' said the guy on the other end.

'To get movie tickets?' Jason asked.

There was a pause, and Jason wondered if the signal had died again. 'Hello?'

'Don't try to be cute,' came the reply. 'You have your deadline. After that I get really upset.'

Jason rolled his eyes. 'Dude, it's Malibu. What is there to be upset about?'

'Malibu?' Laughter filled his ear, and then the guy said, 'Thank you. Remember, thirty-six hours.'

'What are you talking about?' Jason asked. 'Billy?'

But he heard only silence. Jason pulled the phone away from his ear and glanced at the screen. It was empty. The guy had hung up.

'Who were you talking to?' Tyler asked from behind him.

Jason turned and shrugged. 'I thought it was my sister's friend, Billy, but he was being really weird. Maybe it was a wrong number.'

Tyler strode forward and snatched the phone from Jason's hand. 'That's *my* phone, moron,' he snapped. He hit a few buttons, calling up the phone log.

'Excuse me?' Jason said, annoyed. He and Tyler trashed each other a lot, but it was always just joking around. This time Tyler didn't sound amused at all. 'Did you just call me a moron?'

'You told him you were in Malibu,' Tyler said angrily. 'What the hell did you do that for?'

'Because I thought it was Billy,' Jason retorted. 'What was your phone doing on the front seat?'

'It must've fallen out of my pocket when I got out,' Tyler said. 'But I bet Danielle wouldn't appreciate you answering *her* phone, either.'

'She wouldn't go all psycho on me,' Jason said. 'What's your damage?'

'What else did he say?' Tyler demanded.

'He said something about thirty-six hours and about how he'd get upset if you missed the deadline,' Jason replied. 'Now why don't you tell me who that was and what the hell is going on?'

Tyler looked him up and down, his eyes dark with fury. 'You know, man? It's none of your business,' he said. He turned and stalked into the house without another word.

Jason stayed rooted to the spot, replaying that phone conversation in his mind. Clearly the guy on the phone was threatening Tyler. But why? And what was the threat?

Now, at least he was sure of one thing: Dani was right. Tyler was in trouble.

Serious trouble.

EIGHT

At eight o'clock, Jason decided it was time to go talk to Tyler. His friend had vanished into the guest room after their argument out front, and he hadn't come out since. But Zach's party started in half an hour, and Jason wanted to clear the air before that. Besides, he felt Tyler might be in need of a friend and Jason was determined to be there for him – if only he could get past the crap first.

'Ty, you awake?' he called, knocking on the bedroom door. There was no answer, but the door swung open a bit. Jason stuck his head in. 'Tyler?'

The room was empty. Glancing around, Jason spotted Tyler's prescription bottle sitting on the dresser. Except he knew that it wasn't Tyler's prescription – there had been someone else's name on it. Guiltily, he went over to check out the bottle. *Maybe I just read it wrong*, he thought hopefully.

Ryan Swank. That was the name on the label. Not Tyler Deegan. Not even close.

Jason squinted at the rest of the info. There was a doctor's name and a phone number from Detroit. And the name of the medication: Ritalin.

Ritalin. Tyler had said he was taking the medication for pain, but Jason knew Ritalin wasn't a painkiller. It was a drug prescribed for Attention Deficit Disorder, and sometimes used – illegally – by people who wanted to get high.

Tyler didn't have ADD.

Jason's heart sank. Tyler had promised that he was done with the drug-taking. But the fact that he had a bottle full of Ritalin seemed like more than mere coincidence. Jason shook the bottle. He'd only picked it up for a second yesterday, but he was pretty sure it had felt heavier then. It seemed that Tyler had taken some of the pills. *Well that explains his ability to go from exhausted to manic in sixty seconds,* Jason thought grimly. He sighed and put the bottle back down.

Out in the hallway, Jason went over to the bathroom door and pounded on it. 'Tyler, you in there?' he yelled.

'In the shower!' Tyler called back. 'Be out in five.'

Jason hesitated. He'd been worried about taking Tyler to Zach's party before, but now he *really* didn't want to. If Tyler was still taking drugs, there was no telling what he'd do at one of the wild DeVere Heights blowouts.

'Listen, you wanna scratch this party tonight?' he called through the door. 'Maybe hang with Dani and her friend?'

'No way,' Tyler replied. 'Sounds like this party is a primo event.'

Like Tyler would ever turn down a party. Jason couldn't come up with a solid reason why they shouldn't go. He wasn't ready to confront his friend about the drugs. He needed to think about the best way of tackling that one first. In the meantime, he decided he'd have to hope for the best. But he was *not* looking forward to partying with Tyler tonight.

'Have fun,' Dani said, twenty minutes later.

'You could not sound more insincere if you tried,' Jason told her with a grin.

'Don't worry, we'll have a drink for you,' Tyler said as Jason pushed open the front door and stepped out into the cool California night.

'Have two. I'd have two if I were there,' Dani shouted after them.

'Be good at the movies,' Jason called back as she closed the door.

'Why doesn't she just tell your mom she's going to the movies and then come with us?' Tyler asked.

'She did that once,' Jason said. 'And that was the party where someone died.'

'Ouch,' Tyler replied.

'Yeah. I think she's too spooked to try that again.' They got into the Bug and Jason pulled out. He drove slowly down to the main road in DeVere Heights, taking as much time as possible to get to Zach's.

'These parties really as good as Dani says?' Tyler asked, a hint of nervousness in his voice.

'Yeah. It can get pretty wild.' Jason glanced sideways at his friend. 'We can still blow it off if you want.'

'You don't want to take me to your precious party, do you?' Tyler suddenly snapped. 'That's why you're talking about skipping out, right? You're still stuck on that one time I took your car. Just get over it already!'

'Look, you told me you were done with the drugs, but I know you're lying. So who knows what else you're lying about?' Jason retorted. He knew this wasn't the way to broach the subject. He hadn't intended to tackle it at all this evening, but his temper had got the better of him. 'I'm friends with these people, Tyler. I don't want you making an ass of yourself tonight.'

'Well, don't worry. I'm not going to embarrass you in front of your special new friends. I'll be invisible,' Tyler muttered.

Jason took a deep breath and didn't comment on the extreme unlikelihood of Tyler ever being invisible. He'd been arguing with Tyler all afternoon, but he didn't feel angry. He felt worried. 'Ty, listen,' he said. 'What's really going on? I know you're not just here for a visit. You're in some kind of trouble, right?'

'Yeah.' Tyler's voice was so quiet that Jason could barely hear him. 'I'm in big trouble.'

'Well, tell me what it is,' Jason said. 'I can help you.'

'No you can't, Jason,' Tyler said. 'Nobody can help.'

'Whoa. That's pretty negative, dude,' Jason said, surfer-style, hoping to get a smile out of Tyler. It didn't work. 'How do you know I can't help if you don't tell me what's going on?'

'I just know, OK?'

Jason shrugged and focused on the road. He wasn't going to beg the guy.

'Unless your dad's so rich now that you get a couple of thousand as your allowance,' Tyler muttered.

'You need two thousand dollars?' Jason tried to keep the shock out of his voice.

'Five, actually,' Tyler admitted.

Jason let out a long, low whistle. That was a serious lump of cash.

'See, Freeman, there are things even you can't fix,' Tyler said, wiping his hands nervously on the legs of his jeans.

'How'd you get in so deep?' Jason asked. 'Credit card?'

Tyler snorted.

'Betting on b-ball?' Jason suggested. *Would any bookie let Tyler run up that kind of tab?* he wondered. *They'd have to be one stupid illegal businessman.*

'What does it matter?' Tyler sounded pissy now. He always sounded pissy when he was scared. Jason remembered the time Tyler almost got bitten by a rattlesnake on a Boy Scout hiking trip. Well, actually, the time Tyler *saw* a rattlesnake on a Boy Scout hiking trip. He had been so scared that he'd cursed the thing out for two solid minutes, using words in combinations even the Scout Master hadn't heard before.

'I guess I just thought knowing who you owed the money to might help us come up with a plan,' Jason answered.

'Us,' Tyler repeated. 'There is no "us" in this situation. There's just me.'

'Hey, you showed up at my door with a problem.

That means there's an "us".' Jason pulled through the massive iron gates leading to the Lafrenière property. 'So cough it up. How'd you rack up that kind of debt?' He flashed on the bottle of Ritalin in Tyler's room. 'Ritalin?'

'Everyone needs some recreation once in a while,' Tyler answered, without really answering. 'It ain't no big thang.'

A valet in a black suit and a narrow black tie signaled Jason to a stop. Tyler jumped out of the car without waiting for Jason and headed up the long driveway. Jason took the claim check from the valet and followed Tyler, not bothering to hurry. He wasn't eager to get to the party. He was in an even less celebratory mood now than he had been when he left the house. *Some Thanksgiving vacation*, Jason thought. *Let's all give thanks for pissy, drug-abusing friends who won't tell you the whole story about anything, even when you're just trying to help.*

'There are probably five thousand bucks worth of those candle thingies in the trees,' Tyler commented when Jason caught up to him.

'Possibly.' Jason glanced at the trees lining the drive. Hundreds of clear glass globes hung from the branches, and each one held a short fat candle and glowed with golden candlelight. More candles gleamed from the decks and balconies that jutted out on all the levels of the house.

'Where do they get all their cash?' Tyler asked.

'Mom's a screenwriter. Dad's a music producer,' Jason said, wishing Tyler would get off the subject. People in Malibu didn't walk around talking about how much stuff cost or how anybody got the money they had. It was considered tacky.

'So that chick over there who looks like the actress in that cheerleader movie, but skinnier?' Tyler indicated a direction with a slight jerk of his chin. 'That's actually really her?'

Jason tried to look without looking like he was looking. 'I'd say yeah.'

'Do you think she'd like to know that I have a poster of her over my bed?' Tyler joked. 'Or do you think I need a different approach?'

'I'm sure she'd find that truly flattering,' Jason answered as they stepped through the double front doors and into the house. 'She being beautiful and famous. And you being you.'

'I'll hit on her later,' Tyler decided. 'Give her time to watch me from afar and become intrigued.'

'Good idea.'

Tyler headed over to the bar that had been set up in the entryway, complete with babe bartender, who was flipping bottles like she was half-juggler. 'The signature drink of the evening is the pumpkin martini,' she told them. ''Tinis of all sorts are available: apple, chocolate, clean, dirty. And pretty much any other kind of alcohol you want.'

'Only party I've been to where there's not a line by the booze,' Tyler commented.

'Well, you only have to go a few feet to find another bar,' the bartender answered.

'I'll go with the pumpkin.' Tyler grinned at Jason. 'This is definitely the place to come if you want to forget your problems for a few hours.'

Jason thought that over for all of two seconds. Hell, why not? Like Tyler said, it was only for a few hours. There was still time to deal with Tyler's damage post-fun. 'Beer for me.'

'You've got to give me more than that,' the bartender told him.

'Surprise me,' Jason said. She handed him a Heineken. He wasn't sure what that said about him. Maybe just that he hadn't yet completely assimilated to Malibu, home of designer beer.

His eyes swept over what he thought was the living

room. All the furniture had been moved out to make space for dancing and a DJ kept everyone moving with a hip hop/reggae mix. Clips from movies – Adam would probably be able to identify every one – were being projected on one wall. A baby floating in space. Keanu bending under a bullet. Chewbacca roaring. John Travolta disco dancing in a white suit. Mike Myers in a kilt. That freakazoid girl from *The Ring* crawling out of the well.

'So this is your life now, huh?' Tyler asked. He took a sip of his martini.

'Not quite. I still have to take out the trash,' Jason answered.

'Great. Malibu party boy surrounded by excess whines about the one chore he has to do.' Adam approached, his camera stuck to his face. 'I think I have to use this for the trailer.'

'Happy to be of service.' Jason shook his head. 'That thing is going to become permanently grafted to your eye if you don't put it down occasionally. You ever think of, maybe . . . I don't know, leaving it at home?'

'And face the world – and *people* – without my layer of ironic protection?' Adam protested. 'Besides, you never know when a really good docu-drama is going to unfold.'

'Glad you guys could make it,' Zach called over the music. He joined them, shaking hands all around. 'Adam, my mom scored a print of the new Tarantino flick. In the screening room at midnight.'

Adam lowered his camera. 'You,' he said slowly, 'are a god.'

'I have to pass on one rule from my parents,' Zach told them. 'We can do anything we want to the first floor and the basement – short of burning them to the ground – but the top floor is off limits.'

'And you expect us to stay?' Jason joked.

'The pool and the grounds are also available,' Zach told him.

'Oh, well then, I guess we can hang for an hour or so,' Jason said.

'Speak for yourself,' Tyler put in. 'I'm never leaving.'

Zach smiled. 'Let me know if there's anything you want that you can't find,' he said, and headed to the entryway to greet some new arrivals.

'Cool guy,' Tyler commented.

'He was almost chatty,' Adam added. 'Those may have been the most words Lafrenière has ever said to me at one time. I wonder if there's something more mood altering than 'tinis available that our friend's been dipping into.'

Jason shot a glance at Tyler. He hoped *his* friend wouldn't go looking for anything stronger than the drink he had in his hand.

'I think I must have stretched out my stomach with yesterday's gorge,' Adam continued, 'because I'm hungry. In my travels, I saw this phenomenal dessert station. There's actually a chef making Bananas Foster.'

'Do you think they have pumpkin pie?' Tyler asked. 'You know it's not good to mix bananas and pumpkin.' He waved his martini glass. 'That's a recipe for vomit.'

'Are you kidding?' Adam asked as they wove their way across the dance floor. 'Clearly I haven't expressed the scope of this dessert bar. It's monster.' He led the way out to the huge deck that surrounded the pool. The dessert table went on for a mile, the scent of banana liqueur and hot sugar mixing with the salty breeze coming off the ocean.

'Check it,' Tyler said.

Jason watched as the chef scooped up a ladle of liquid from around some simmering bananas and torched it. He poured it back into the pan – a stream of fire that hit the bananas with a whoosh of blue flame.

'Wait. I hear my name. Someone's calling me.' Adam headed toward the chef.

Tyler snagged a piece of pumpkin pie, and Jason decided on a brownie with caramel on the top.

As he picked it up, he heard Sienna's familiar laugh. And for a second, he felt like he'd had a six-pack instead of just one beer. He turned and spotted her with Belle, reclining on matching lounge chairs on the other side of the pool. Van Dyke stood next to them.

Jason wandered – in what he hoped looked like a casual way – in their direction. Tyler followed him.

Sienna laughed when she spotted them. 'Uh-oh. We're being invaded by Michigan.'

'I'm not complaining,' Belle purred.

'Remember that the extremely jealous boyfriend is probably lurking nearby,' Jason warned under his breath. Tyler nodded.

'Pretty soon there are going to be more of you than there are of us,' Sienna teased.

'And that would be a bad thing?' Jason asked. 'You could use some good Midwestern stock in the mix. You've got soft out here.'

'Soft? Feel this!' Sienna reached out, grabbed Jason's hand, and ran his fingers across her taut abs. Jason tried to look unimpressed.

'Gym muscles,' Tyler scoffed. 'Those don't count. Jason and I have real muscles, from working the land.'

'Yeah, Jason, I'm sure you worked the land every weekend – mowing the lawn,' Sienna joked.

Van Dyke and Belle laughed.

'You don't get muscles like this mowing the lawn.' Jason retorted. He caught Sienna's hand, flexed, and pressed it against his bicep. He knew he shouldn't be doing it. He knew he should be keeping his hands off her. *But it's not like we're going behind Brad's back or anything*, he told himself. *We're just two friends, joking around, in front of loads of people.*

Right.

'Ooooh.' Sienna gave his arm a little squeeze. 'You're right! You definitely don't get muscles like that mowing the lawn. You must have had one of those mowers you ride on.'

'Meow!' Belle said, grinning at Sienna.

'Just give up,' Van Dyke suggested to Jason.

'Yes. I'm too smart for you.' Sienna sighed, her dark eyes flashing with mischief.

Jason raised an eyebrow. 'You won't seem so smart when you're dripping wet,' he remarked, with a nod to the pool. He turned back to Sienna. 'Watch it. Or you're going in.'

'With those muscles? I don't think so,' Sienna shot back, laughing.

She was asking for it.

Jason lunged toward her lounge chair and Sienna leaped out of it with a shriek and darted away.

Let her go, Jason told himself. But he couldn't. And as he raced after her, Jason realized that Sienna was his Ritalin. And he was an addict. The high he got being around her was just too damn *high* to give up.

'Jason, I'm going to break the kegstand record. I'm going for a full minute,' Harberts called as Jason headed toward him. He flipped onto his hands, and two guys grabbed his legs. Erin Henry positioned the keg tap in Harberts' mouth and flipped it.

'One, two, three—' the crowd around him began to chant as Harberts struggled to force beer up his throat.

Sienna had disappeared into the house. Jason picked up speed, dodging the stream of beer Harberts had just started to spew, and running into the den. A group of guys from the football team were lounging on the over-stuffed leather couches, watching a Super Bowl game on the plasma-screen TV. Sienna was disappearing through another door, so Jason followed.

He found himself in a home gym, fully equipped. Weight machines, cardio machines, a lap pool, and Sienna. She was bouncing on a trampoline, her hair flying around her, her cheeks flushed.

Jason walked towards her. 'Don't think I'm not going to carry you right back out to that pool,' he warned.

'You'll have to catch me first,' Sienna taunted, jumping lightly off the trampoline and disappearing through another door.

'Right,' Jason muttered, picking up speed again. He ran out into the corridor, in time to see a door close. Throwing it open he saw the library beyond and, for a split second, he thought he'd found Sienna. But when the girl turned toward him, he saw it was Lauren Gissinger. She sat with Dominic and two other guys, playing poker – strip poker. Lauren was clearly bra-less under her thin T-shirt, and one of the guys was shirtless – except for a lacy pink and black bra. *Must be some rule I don't know about!* Jason thought.

'Wanna play?' Lauren asked.

'Maybe later,' Jason muttered as he heard Sienna laugh behind him and whirled around to see her at the other end of the corridor. He followed her into a sun room. It had glass on three sides, plants all around and lots of bamboo furniture. The air felt dense with oxygen.

Sienna darted behind a sofa – like that was enough to stop him. Jason leaped straight over the back.

'Nowhere to run,' he told Sienna, strolling lazily toward her.

Sienna backed away, laughing and reaching behind her for the balcony doors. She got the handle, twisted it and slipped outside. Jason was out the door half a second later.

The small balcony had a wrought-iron railing all the way around it. Candles illuminated it, casting golden light on Sienna's face. She was close now and Jason could hear her breath coming fast. He smiled as she backed up again – and hit the railing.

Jason grabbed the rail on either side of her, creating a wall with his body. Sienna twisted back and forth, trying to wriggle away.

'Now what were you saying about my muscles?' Jason asked as she gave him a playful push that didn't move him an inch.

'That they're very strong and manly,' Sienna lied with a grin.

'That's not what I remember.' Jason moved closer, preparing to drag her back to the pool. But he didn't want to take her back out to the crowd. He wanted to stay right there with her – alone.

He stared into her dark eyes, then Sienna's arms came up around his neck and her body met his. Just like in his dream, her lips parted . . . and, suddenly, the rest of the dream came flooding back. Jason remembered Sienna's eyes – unrecognizable and full of bloodlust. He drew back, needing to look into her eyes again, needing to know that she was still Sienna and not someone – or some*thing* – else.

NINE

Sienna looked up at Jason in surprise as he drew back. Her dark eyes were wide with confusion. There was no bloodlust. There were no fangs. There was just Sienna looking puzzled and then pissed off.

'Sienna, I—' Jason began, trying to explain.

But it was too late.

'Forget it,' Sienna said flatly, and she turned and walked away. Just walked. The chase was over. Jason knew he'd screwed up. He'd had her. She'd wanted him to kiss her. But he'd flashed back to his dream and . . . well, that was that.

If I could just explain, he thought. Yeah. Just say 'Sienna, I wasn't trying to give you mixed signals or mess you around. I completely want to kiss you. It's just that for one minute I thought about this nightmare where you gave in to the bloodlust and attacked me.' Right. That would work.

But he had to do something. Jason pulled in a deep

breath, combed his hair with his fingers, and smoothed down his shirt. Then he retraced his steps. Sienna wasn't in the library. Neither were Erin or Dominic. The two remaining guys had switched over to playing for cash. Jason saw a couple of fifties lying on the table.

He returned to the gym. Vivian Andersen was lying on the trampoline now, staring up at the ceiling and giggling, like there was a movie up there or something. No Sienna.

Jason skirted the glossy polished floor of the basketball court and headed into the den. His heart twisted painfully in his chest, because there was Sienna. On one of the leather couches. More specifically, on Brad's lap on one of the leather couches.

Sienna caught Jason's eye, her gaze ice. Then she took Brad's face in her hands, leaned down and kissed him – long and deep. The kiss that should have been Jason's, *would* have been Jason's if he hadn't screwed up so spectacularly.

Jason abruptly turned away. He didn't want to see what he was missing. And besides, he didn't want anyone to realize how he felt about Sienna.

He headed toward the pool, just to have a destination. Belle and Van Dyke passed him. '. . . to get up to the Garden,' Van Dyke was saying. Jason tried to put a smile – or at least a normal, relaxed expression – on his face. They didn't notice him, and he felt relieved. He didn't want to try to come up with words right now. He sat down in the closest deck chair and stared vacantly at the water volleyball game that had started up in his absence.

A few minutes later, Adam sat down in the chair next to him. 'Remember what I said about not knowing when a docu-drama was going to unfold?' he asked.

Jason nodded.

'Well, the unfolding is happening now, I'm pretty sure,' Adam went on. 'There's this slow migration happening. People are heading upstairs – where no one is supposed to go.'

Jason shrugged. 'Ever been to a party where that *doesn't* happen?'

'Mia Hodges' third birthday party. Because we were all afraid of Mrs Hodges,' Adam answered. 'But it's not just regular people going upstairs. It's only people of the Sienna, Zach, Brad type.'

Meaning vampires. 'So they're having themselves a little sub-party,' Jason said.

'Could be,' Adam agreed. 'Could be something else. Don't you want to know why they all suddenly have this need to get together?'

'If they want to be alone, let them be,' Jason replied with a shrug. Right now, he was just happy to know that Sienna and Brad were going to be out of sight for a while.

Adam frowned. 'Do you remember putting on some kind of metal hat? Maybe some electricity?' he asked. 'Because I think somebody may have switched our brains. Aren't you the guy who was more suspicious of our *friends* than I was?'

'Yeah,' Jason admitted. 'But the way Zach handled the Luke Archer thing made me think that we can basically trust them to deal with their own crap. I don't know about you, but I have enough of my own to deal with.' Thinking of Sienna. And Brad. And Tyler.

'I just want to take a little peek. Come on.' Adam got to his feet, slinging his camera strap over his shoulder. 'I know where there's a back staircase.'

'Adam, it's not our business what they're—'

But Adam was gone. Jason closed his eyes for a long moment. Then he opened them and headed after his friend. He couldn't let the guy go up there alone.

Jason spotted Belle and Van Dyke walking up the main staircase as he followed Adam. 'We're going to have to be careful or we're going to get spotted,' Jason warned when he caught up to Adam at the smaller staircase off the kitchen.

'Careful is nothing like my middle name, which is Tecumseh. But, yeah,' Adam answered, starting up the stairs. He slowed down as they reached the top. Jason peered over his shoulder. There was nothing to see but empty hallway. And nothing to hear but the dull thud of the music from the party.

'If we're doing this, now's a good time,' Jason said. He and Adam headed down the hall. Adam paused outside a closed door, listened for a moment, then swung the door open. A bedroom. Probably a guest room. Nothing too personal in it. Empty.

Adam shut the door and they continued. Another bedroom. Also empty. They moved on to the upstairs living room, just off the main staircase. Empty.

'Something mysterious has occurred,' Adam said, turning on the camera and panning across the empty sofas and chairs. 'My colleague and I witnessed people coming upstairs. But having followed them, we've found nobody.' Adam pointed the camera at Jason. 'What are your theories?'

'I thought I told you not to come up here,' someone interrupted before Jason could answer.

Jason turned to see Zach Lafrenière standing in the doorway. He didn't look happy.

TEN

Where the hell did Zach come from? Jason wondered. 'Sorry. Uh, the line for the head downstairs is almost out the front door,' he said quickly. 'It was piss on the rosebushes or come up here.'

'And the rosebushes, they have thorns,' Adam added, lowering his camera. 'Not safe. My future wife may want children.'

Zach raised one dark eyebrow, and Jason suddenly felt like a five-year-old. Make that a five-year-old with a bright purple tongue being all 'Grape popsicles! What grape popsicles? I haven't seen any grape popsicles!'

'There are four bathrooms down there,' Zach said, one corner of his mouth lifting in amusement. 'Come on. I'll give you the tour. I think you'll especially enjoy the one off my dad's office. The toilet has a heated seat.' He turned and headed for the stairs.

'I don't think I've ever heard Lafrenière make a joke

115

before,' Adam said under his breath as he and Jason followed Zach downstairs.

'Down that hallway. Third door on the left,' Zach said when they reached the first floor.

'Thanks,' Jason answered.

Zach turned and loped back upstairs.

'He sounded downright cheerful. And he was grinning!' Adam exclaimed. 'Now I really want to know what's going on with the vampires. I know it's his birthday, but come on. What could be happening up there to put Zach in such a great mood?'

'Vampire Bingo?' Jason suggested.

'Don't be an ass,' Adam said. 'Seriously, what do you think they're all doing right now? They can't be having some private feeding session. They'd need humans for that.'

Jason nodded thoughtfully.

'Do you think they're planning something?' Adam went on. 'Something that made Lafrenière so happy that he actually smiled?'

Jason wished Adam would drop the topic. Whatever they were doing, he figured it was *their* business – as in, *not Adam's*. 'Vampire square dancing!' he said firmly.

'Definitely a complete ass,' Adam retorted.

'Wanna check out the bowling alley? Get some footage?' Jason started down the hallway. 'Because, really, can you even name one truly great film that does not include a bowling scene?'

'*The Bicycle Thief*,' Adam answered, falling into step beside him.

'I said truly great,' Jason protested. He led the way into the basement: five bowling lanes with electronic scoring, vintage video games, two pool tables, jukebox with accompanying disco ball and strobe lights, and Tikki bar. Not your regular rec room. In fact, not your non-multi-billionaire rec room.

But even with all the toys, without the vampires – meaning without the most popular of the popular – there was something missing from the party. Some kind of . . . shimmer. Or maybe it was just lack of Sienna that was making the party feel flat to Jason.

Which meant his whole life was going to be feeling flat from now on, he reflected, because Jason got the impression that Sienna didn't plan on being around him much ever again.

In the middle of his second bowling match, Jason caught sight of Sienna just as he released the ball. So the vampires had returned. Jason forced his attention to the pins and watched his ball take out all but two: a seven-ten split. Nasty.

'Goal posts!' Harberts yelled. 'That's a shot for you, my friend.' He handed Jason a shot glass of tequila.

Nasty, but not without benefits, Jason thought. He downed the shot. The sensation was not unlike staring into Sienna's eyes: a long burst of fire from mouth to gut.

Sienna looked away, wrapping her arms around Brad, and Jason felt cold in spite of the tequila. Seeing Sienna all over Brad sucked the pleasure out of everything.

Jason didn't want to be there anymore. He worked it out carefully in his head: one beer when they'd first arrived, and now one shot – he was OK to drive. He wondered where Tyler was. He hadn't seen the guy in hours.

'You took your shot. Now take your shot,' Harberts told him.

Jason grabbed the closest bowling ball, sent it down the lane without aiming, and managed to knock down one of the remaining pins. He decided to name it Brad. Even though Brad was a decent guy and had done nothing to deserve being slammed to the ground by a bowling ball – except be lucky enough to have Sienna as his girlfriend.

'Take over for me,' Jason called to Craig Yoder, a guy from his history class.

'You've got some catching up to do.' Harberts tossed Craig the blue Cabo Wabo bottle as Jason made his way over to the stairs. He took them three at a time and followed the sound of whoops and whistles through the house and out onto the back patio. Tyler usually managed to locate – if not create – the epicenter of a party. It seemed like the place to start the search. Maybe he'd find Adam too. He'd wandered off after the first game of bowling ended.

No Tyler on the patio. Although Jason thought his friend would have liked to be there if he could see Belle right that second. She was shaking her money-maker down the top of the adobe wall that ran around the courtyard. Guys lined the wall below her, arms up. Wanting to be the one who caught her if she fell.

Dominic stood at the edge of the crowd, arms crossed over his chest, watching Belle and her entourage, blue eyes narrow. Did any of those guys realize an armful of Belle almost certainly came with a gutful of her boyfriend's fists? Jason wondered.

He made his way deeper into the backyard and over

to the pool. What Michigan boy wouldn't want to be hanging in an outdoor pool in November? Especially when Maggie Roy was floating on a lounge chair in the center, her long, golden-brown hair trailing in the water.

As Jason watched, Maggie used her fingertips to slowly paddle down to the shallow end of the pool and over to Kyle Priesmeyer, one of the divers on the swim team. She reached up, looped her hands around his neck and pulled his head down for a kiss. The lounge chair rocked, but didn't capsize, and Kyle stretched out on top of Maggie.

Jason knew that Maggie had begun to feed on Kyle. And the guy was oblivious. To anything but the pleasure. Jason shook his head and continued his search for Tyler.

He hurried back into the house to check the kitchen. At most parties Jason went to, there was a solid party-within-a-party in the kitchen. Probably because people went in looking for a beer, or whatever, and just stayed.

Yep. There was indeed a sub-party in the kitchen, which included Adam, eating a slice of white pizza and trying to explain why reincarnation was complete bull. It was the kind of convo that you could only have really effectively while blotto. There was still no Tyler.

'Jason, back me up here,' Adam called, waving him toward the group. 'A whole buttload of people would have to be walking around soulless for reincarnation to be possible, correct? Because if there are a finite number of souls that keep coming back, and no new ones, there aren't enough souls to go around, because of population growth.'

'Have you seen Tyler?' Jason asked, ignoring the question.

'But, no,' a girl with bangs and an intense expression said. 'All the souls available aren't inhabiting bodies all the time. The number of people on earth thousands of years ago tells you nothing about the total number of souls. There's no correlation.'

'Tyler?' Jason said again.

'Haven't seen him since before we went upstairs,' Adam answered. He broke away from the group and crossed over to Jason. 'But you know what I *have* seen?' He lowered his voice. 'A lot of our special friends circling around Zach.'

'You can see that every day at school,' Jason pointed out. Zach was pretty much the top of the DeVere High food chain.

'It's more than the usual Zach-adoration. And it's more than him being the birthday boy,' Adam said, taking a bite of his pizza. 'And he's still smiling. And the smiles are somehow vampire-related, because whatever is making him smile, they all know about it.'

'Huh,' Jason said, not wanting to encourage Adam.

'Yeah. Big huh.' Adam tossed his pizza crust in the trash. 'And even though I know the vampires have funded a massive percentage of our Malibu goodness, it kind of freaks me out to think of them behind closed doors, making plans. I mean, shouldn't our kind have a delegation?'

Jason shrugged. 'If they're planning their annual croquet tournament, no. If they're coming up with, uh—' He glanced around to make sure no one was listening, 'some kind of meal plan, yeah. But remember, Zach and company totally handled Luke Archer.'

'Yeah. They stepped up,' Adam agreed. 'I guess I should—'

'Adam, did you consider the animal and insect population in your theory?' Saunders Graydon, a junior in desperate need of a growth spurt, called.

'Insects? So every mosquito has a soul, is that what you're telling me?' Adam asked, returning to the debate.

'I'm going to keep looking for Tyler,' Jason muttered. He grabbed a Hanson's kiwi and strawberry soda on his way out. The first time he'd encountered it, it had sounded kind of repulsive. But now he was getting addicted.

He took a swig as he headed for the family room. Sometime during the party, it had become make-out central. He did a Tyler scan. Didn't see him. Jason turned away. But then, through the sliding doors leading to one of the house's many decks, he thought he saw a flash of dark blue sweatshirt, like the one Tyler had been wearing tied around his waist.

Jason hurried across the room, careful not to step on the couple stretched out in front of the fire. He was still getting used to the fact that in Malibu, sixty-five degrees was considered fireplace weather.

He opened the door and saw Tyler leaning against the deck's wooden railing, staring down at the ocean. 'There you are,' Jason said. 'I've been looking for you.'

Tyler whipped around. 'Oh, hey.'

Jason shook his head. 'You haven't even been here a week, and you're going native.'

'What?' Tyler asked.

'You've got your hoodie zipped up to your neck like it's freezing,' Jason said.

'Ocean makes it cold out here,' Tyler answered, his hands jammed into the front pockets.

'What are you doing out here by yourself anyway? I was looking for you in the party hot spots. You know, the Tyler zones.'

'I wasn't out here *by myself* until a few minutes ago,' Tyler said. He turned toward the ocean, then immediately turned back to face Jason. 'You know what I mean? Huh? Huh? Huh, huh, huh?'

Jason laughed. 'So who was she?'

'It wasn't a name kind of situation,' Tyler replied.

'Well, what'd she look like?' Jason asked. *Did she have anything unusual about her?* he added silently. *Like fangs?*

'What? You're not getting any, so you need to live through me? Is that it?'

Jason decided that it didn't seem like Tyler had been fed on. He was talking fast, and his eyes were darting back and forth. After Erin had sucked on him at Belle's party, Jason remembered that he had hardly been able to move. He'd felt drunk and floaty, and, to be all California surfer about it, mellow. Tyler definitely didn't have a mellow on.

But had there even been a girl out here with him? Jason wondered darkly. Or had Tyler been hanging out with his friend Ritalin? Was that why he was all twitchy?

'You ready to get out of here?' Tyler asked.

'Sure.' Jason had thought he might have to pry Tyler out of the party with a crowbar. His friend was a stay-'til-the-last-beer-then-go-get-more kind of guy. He was glad he didn't have to persuade Tyler to leave. But it did put some more checks in the Tyler weirdness column. 'Let's go tell Adam we're heading out.'

Jason led the way back to the kitchen. The reincarnation talk had switched over to – with Adam in the group, what else? – movies.

'We're thinking about taking off,' Jason told him.

'You're not staying for the screening? We're talking Tarantino here. Are you feverish?' Adam asked.

'Nah. Just like to leave the party at the peak,' Jason told him. It didn't really make sense, but whatever. 'See you at school.'

'See you,' Adam said.

As they got close to the front door, Jason spotted Sienna and Brad lingering in the hallway, standing close together. His heart suddenly felt as if it had tripled in weight. 'See you guys later,' Jason forced himself to say.

'You're leavin'?' Brad asked. 'Mistake. The party second wind is about to hit. I can feel it.'

Sienna didn't say a word. She didn't even look at

Jason as he slapped hands with Brad and made his way out the door.

Tyler hurried toward the Bug, his hands still shoved in his pockets. Jason followed him. He glanced back once, and saw Sienna kissing Brad again, her hands sliding up under his shirt.

She could drink every drop of blood in my body if she kissed me like that to do it, Jason thought. *And I'd die happy . . .*

ELEVEN

'OK, boys, spill!' Aunt Bianca ordered Jason and Tyler the next morning. 'What kind of depravity went on at that party last night?'

Stellar. The last thing Jason wanted to talk about was the party. All it was to him was the site of his screw-up with Sienna. And Tyler was no help. He just sat there gazing at his sausages as if they held the secrets of the universe. His foot, propped on the chair leg, bounced about a million miles an hour.

'That juicy, hmm?' Bianca asked. 'You can't even come up with one thing you're willing to share?'

'Bowling,' Jason answered. He scooped a second helping of scrambled eggs out of the frying pan and onto to his plate, then sat back down at the kitchen table. 'You know, it's a gateway activity. A high percentage of teens who've tried it move on to miniature golf. And once you go there, you can't get back without rehab.'

'Bowling? You left *Zach's* party to go bowling?' Dani shook her head in disgust.

'The Lafrenières have a bowling alley,' Jason said. 'We didn't have to leave.'

Tyler suddenly looked up and rolled an orange across the table, knocking over the salt and pepper shakers. They all stared at him.

'Bowling,' he explained.

Man, the guy was hyper. Had he been popping – or snorting or whatever his ingestion method of choice was – before breakfast? Jason wondered. He glanced around the table. No one else seemed to think Tyler's behavior was strange.

'It's a good thing you stayed home, Dani,' Bianca said. 'That's no kind of environment for you.'

'You're way too young to start with the bowling,' Jason's father agreed with a smile.

'And bowling was the naughtiest thing you got up to?' Aunt Bianca asked, spreading strawberry jam on a piece of toast.

'Pretty much,' Jason answered. What did she think? That he was going to start talking about underage drinking? Or give an estimate on the number of hook-ups that took place at Zach's? Or say that Tyler was probably high by the end of the night and was possibly tweaking right now?

Bianca turned to Tyler. 'Jason's being discreet. *You* tell us about the party. How did it compare to one of your Michigan blasts?'

'It's no different, right, Tyler?' Dani asked.

'No one ended up dead at the parties in Michigan,' Mrs Freeman pointed out, standing up abruptly and refilling her coffee cup.

'Someone *died* at a party out here?' Aunt Bianca asked, stopping with her toast halfway to her mouth. She glanced at Dani. 'You didn't tell me that!'

'It was a party on a yacht. A girl fell overboard and drowned. She'd been drinking,' Jason's mother explained. 'Now do you understand why I don't want Danielle at these things?'

Carrie was already dead when she hit the water, Jason thought, flashing on her body lying on the beach. Her lips blue. Eyes staring sightlessly.

'I . . . I can't believe it,' Aunt Bianca murmured.

'Horrible. I can't even think about her poor parents,' Mrs Freeman said with a shudder.

'Well, last night's party was just a party,' Tyler said. He used his fingers to pop a Tater Tot into his mouth, then another. He swallowed them, hardly bothering to chew, then smiled at Jason's mom. 'The big difference was that the girls were wearing less clothes than they would have been in Michigan.'

Mrs Freeman actually laughed. Tyler had always been good at making her laugh. Jason's dad snorted.

Tyler grabbed the ketchup bottle, opened it and thumped on the bottom so hard that he almost completely smothered his remaining taters. 'I even saw a bikini top floating in the hot tub,' he added. Then he pointed at Bianca with a grin. 'And that's all you're getting out of me.'

'Did you go in the hot tub?' Dani asked casually.

Jason knew what she really wanted to ask Tyler: 'Did you have anything to do with the removal of the bikini top?' Dani could never resist gossip – especially where someone she knew might be involved.

'Didn't bring a bathing suit,' Tyler replied. He looked over at Jason. 'Hey, man. Think you could drive me into town when you're done?'

'Done now,' Jason said, forking the last bite of eggs into his mouth. 'Let's go.' He got up feeling relieved. It would get him away from any more questions about the party.

'I'll meet you out there,' Tyler said. 'I want to grab my jacket.'

'You're not going to need it,' Jason told him, but Tyler was already gone.

Jason stood up and checked his pocket for his car keys. 'See you guys later,' he told his family as he headed out of the kitchen.

He hurried outside, unlocked the car, and slid into the driver's seat. A minute later, Tyler got in, hoodie zipped to his chin. 'Any particular place in town you want to go?' Jason asked.

'Just Malibu central. I'm guessing I'll be able to find a post office there?' Tyler replied.

'Sure.' Jason backed out of the driveway and headed for the Pacific Coast Highway. The view still knocked him out. All that blue ocean stretching out forever. But he noticed that Tyler wasn't looking at the beach. He was staring straight ahead, eyes intense, like he was willing the car to go faster.

'Not like I'm trying to get rid of you, but won't it take you a few days to get home if you have to hitch? And even with those free days at school . . .' Jason let his words trail off. 'I could spot you bus money. Again, not that I'm trying to get rid of you.' Except that he was. Kind of. And how alternate universe was that? Jason wanting Tyler gone? He used to wish the guy was his brother so he could live with the Freemans all the time.

'School's the least of my problems,' Tyler said as Jason turned onto a road peppered with stores. 'You can just let me out here.'

'Here?' Jason glanced at the trendy restaurants and the shoe store. 'You sure?'

'Yeah. Here is good.' Tyler started to swing the door open before Jason had even pulled all the way over to the curb.

'You want to meet up in a while?' Jason asked. It was more than obvious that Tyler didn't want Jason anywhere around right now.

'I'll find my own way back,' Tyler said as he climbed out of the car. 'Later.' And he slammed the door before Jason could get another question in.

'Thank you for using Jason's cab service,' Jason muttered, staring after his friend. What was his deal? What did he have planned that he didn't want Jason to know about?

Whatever. Jason couldn't do much if Tyler wasn't going to talk to him. He pulled back out onto the street and made a U-turn at the corner. He spotted Sienna coming out of *L'Occitane en Provence*. Sienna and Belle.

Without giving himself enough time to wimp out, Jason pulled into the parking space just vacated by an

SUV. 'Hey,' he called as he got out of the car. 'Impressive moves on that wall last night, Belle.' He figured it was safer to say something to Belle first. Belle was always friendly.

'I made a couple hundred in tips,' she joked. 'Cold, hard cash. But Dom wasn't happy. He doesn't get that I just like attention. Is that so horrible?'

'I vote no,' Jason said. 'So what are you two up to?'

'I just bought some Olive Paste. It's the best thing in the world for sun-damaged hair,' Belle told him. 'Sienna's keeping me company. Not that she's actually talking or anything.'

'I've talked,' Sienna protested.

'Right. You said the words "venti mochachino" about half an hour ago,' Belle teased.

'Half an hour ago?' Jason repeated. 'Then you must be ready for another one. I know shopping for hair products is thirsty work.' That sounded kind of dumb. 'Not that I spend much time shopping for hair products,' he added, which didn't sound any better.

He figured dumb didn't matter. All that mattered was that he got to spend some time with Sienna. Enough time so that she'd actually start speaking to him again. Possibly even want to kiss him again in this lifetime.

'No, Belle needs to get home,' Sienna said. She seemed to be talking to his left ear. 'She insisted on wearing her new Jimmy Choos and she's destroyed her feet.'

'I'll drop you at your car,' Jason offered gallantly, thinking that even that would give him a little Sienna time. 'Where'd you park?'

'We walked,' Belle answered. 'Not my most intelligent decision, I admit.' She shook her head at her sandals, which were nothing but some thin straps and spike heels.

'I'll drive you home, then,' Jason said firmly. Score. He'd drop Belle off first, then—

'Oooh. Yes, please,' Belle said, pulling Jason away from his thoughts. She slipped off the sandals and picked them up.

'Do you mind if I don't come with you?' Sienna asked Belle. 'I said I'd drop in at Brad's place and help his mom pick out new drapes. I'll call and have Brad pick me up.' She looked Jason in the eye for the first time. 'I'd rather not put you out.'

Or be anywhere near you, Jason added silently. He could read between the lines. Message received and understood.

'Sure. Don't let my feet spoil the rest of the day for

you,' Belle said, seeming oblivious to the conversation going on under the conversation. She turned to Jason. 'Can we go? This pavement is getting hot on my poor little piggies.'

What could he say? 'Sure.' He opened the passenger door of the Bug, and Belle hopped in. Jason shut the door for her.

'Sienna, about what happened at the party . . .' he began. He had to take a shot at making things right.

She pulled out her cell and hit a speed-dial number. 'Hey, babe,' she said, looking right at Jason. 'Want to come get me?'

Jason gave a nod, then walked around to the driver's side of the car and slid behind the wheel. 'Thanks so much. You are such the lifesaver,' Belle told him. But Jason wasn't really listening.

You knew Sienna was with Brad. You've known it since the day you met her, Jason told himself. *It's better this way. Let her stay pissed at you. You shouldn't be going after her anyway. Brad's a great guy. Your friend.*

'Where's that Tyler?' Belle asked. 'All the girls at the party were intrigued. Some of them are planning a hunting trip to Michigan, which now seems to be Land of Cute Boys.'

'He's still in town . . . someplace,' Jason told her. *Doing who in the hell knows what*, he thought.

'Did he have fun at his first Malibu party? Zach's was definitely the one to go to.'

'He claimed to. He disappeared for a while, which is usually a sign of some kind of fun, right?' Jason asked, grinning.

'Absolutely. I love to disappear at parties. It makes Dominic go mental, but the best amusements happen away from the crowd,' Belle answered.

They drove past the police station, and Jason thought about Adam: 'Child of the poor but hardworking Chief of Police', as Adam had described himself on the day they met. Maybe he was right. Maybe something had been going on last night with the vampires that at least a few humans should be aware of. And Belle knew Jason was in on the truth about exactly who lived in DeVere Heights.

'I noticed you and Sienna and some of the others disappeared upstairs for a while too,' Jason said, trying to sound casual. 'Were you having fun?'

'Yes.'

Jason thought it was the first time he'd ever heard Belle give a one-word answer to a question. She didn't say anything else for the rest of the ride.

Clearly whatever the vampires had going was nothing humans were allowed to know about. But, like Jason kept telling Adam, that didn't mean it was anything bad. Or any of their business. Right?

TWELVE

Jason noticed it as soon as he walked into the locker room for swim practice on the Monday after Thanksgiving weekend. Something was wrong. It was way too quiet. The guys on the swim team were all there, as usual. But everyone was getting changed silently. There was none of the usual post-school, pre-practice banter.

'What's up with you guys?' Jason called. 'You all still in a turkey coma?'

'One of us is a thief,' Harberts answered flatly.

'What?' Jason demanded, wandering over to Harberts' locker. Brad sat next to him, swim goggles pushed up on his forehead.

'The Lafrenières got robbed the night of Zach's party,' Brad explained.

'They're sure somebody who was at the party did it,' Van Dyke added from the next row of lockers over.

Jason relaxed a tiny bit. 'So you're talking one of us who was there, not one of us on the team,' he said.

'It better not be somebody from the team!' Van Dyke declared, appearing from around the corner. 'That would be an even bigger betrayal.'

'What was taken?' Jason asked. 'A lot?'

'Just one thing. An antique that's been in the Lafrenière family for hundreds of years,' Brad said. 'Zach's dad had a full-on freak this morning when he realized it was missing. He called the school and had Zach yanked from class.'

'That's asinine. What's Zach supposed to do about it?' Harberts asked.

Brad shrugged.

'All I can say is that Maggie Roy is not guilty,' Kyle volunteered, joining the group. 'I had my hands on her all night.'

'Priesmeyer just wants everyone to know that he finally got a little,' Van Dyke commented with a laugh.

'Hey, we're talking Maggie Roy,' Kyle said.

'Been there. Done that,' Harberts told him.

'You lie. We all know you're on your way to being the next forty-year-old virgin,' Scott shot back.

Ah, this was the locker room Jason knew and loved.

'What kind of antique are we talking?' Harberts asked, getting serious again.

'A gold chalice. That's a cup to you, Harberts,' Brad

answered. 'The guy was smart, too. The chalice was locked in Mr Lafrenière's briefcase. I guess the thing is usually kept in a safe deposit box, but he'd taken it out to use over the holiday. Anyway, the thief managed to crack the lock, and he left this glass paperweight in place of the chalice. Otherwise, Mr Lafrenière would have realized something was wrong the second he picked up the case.'

An image of Tyler suddenly slammed into Jason's head. Tyler all twitchy. Hoodie zipped up to his chin. Hands jammed in the big front pocket. Because he was holding the chalice? Hiding it under the baggy sweatshirt?

A year ago, Jason would never have considered the possibility. In fact, he'd have punched anyone who considered the possibility. But since his parents' divorce, Tyler had changed. And he was desperate for cash.

But *that* desperate? Jason wasn't sure.

Then he remembered the phone call. The one on Tyler's cell, with the guy who mentioned a thirty-six hour deadline. The one that had turned Tyler into an instant asshole. It had been an obvious threat. It might have been enough to make Tyler willing to do just about anything.

But the threat was nothing compared to what Tyler

might be facing now. That guy on the phone was human. The ones who'd been robbed were not.

'How can a place like the Lafrenières' not have some extreme hi-tech security system?' Kyle asked.

Brad turned toward Jason, even though the question had been Kyle's. 'It does. There are cameras everywhere. By now, they probably know who did it.'

Jason stared back at him. Was Brad trying to tell him something? Had Brad seen something that made him suspect Tyler, too?

Was it a warning?

'Damn! I completely forgot I have a dentist appointment,' Jason exclaimed. 'My mom's going to massacre me. Tell the coach, OK?'

Brad nodded. And Jason headed out of the locker room, holding himself to a fast walk. The second he was through the doors, he broke into a run. He had to talk to Tyler. He just hoped the guy was in front of the TV where Jason had left him that morning.

Jason raced to the parking lot and over to the Bug. He vaulted into the convertible without bothering to open the door and squealed out of the lot. He pushed his foot down on the accelerator as soon as he hit the PCH. Seventy. Eighty. He needed to find Tyler fast.

Zach Lafrenière was a guy who took action. When

Luke Archer had gone feral, the other vampires had turned to Zach. And Zach had taken care of the problem by driving a metal stake through Luke's heart. What exactly would Zach do to Tyler for stealing something irreplaceable from his family?

Jason caught sight of a figure out of the corner of his eye and slammed on the brakes. He twisted around. Yeah, it was Tyler. His friend was staring at him from the edge of the cliffs overlooking the beach on the other side of the road. 'Tyler!' he shouted. 'Get in the car!'

Tyler waited for a Jeep to drive past, then jogged across the two-lane highway. 'Hey. Decided to walk into town,' he said cheerfully.

'Get in,' Jason told him again.

'I was thinking of maybe renting a board. Can't come all the way to Malibu without at least attempting to surf. Am I right?' Tyler asked.

'The Lafrenières were robbed at the party on Friday,' Jason told him. He locked eyes with Tyler. 'I think it might be a good time for you to be at home. A stranger in town could be at the top of their list of suspects.'

Tyler nodded wordlessly and climbed into the car.

'Did you do it, Ty?' Jason couldn't stop himself from

asking the question. He pulled back onto the highway. He wanted to get Tyler out of sight until he knew exactly what the situation was. 'I don't hear you answering.'

'You take me to a party with you and you think I walk out with something?' Tyler shook his head sadly.

'That's not an answer.' Why couldn't Tyler just give him a 'no'? That was all Jason wanted.

'You have a Bible? I need a Bible if you're going to put me on the witness stand,' Tyler snapped.

Jason glanced at his old friend. He looked as pissed off as he sounded. And Jason wondered if he was wrong. Maybe he'd jumped to a completely false conclusion.

'I didn't do it,' Tyler told him, speaking slowly and carefully, like a kindergarten teacher giving safety instructions. 'Happy?'

'Ecstatic,' Jason muttered as they entered the Heights. 'Sorry,' he told Tyler. 'I just . . .' He didn't go on. There was no explanation good enough for accusing his friend of being a thief.

'Forget it,' Tyler said.

Jason pulled into his driveway – and hit the brakes fast. His stomach seized up as he looked at the house. The front door hung open.

'Didn't my mom and Bianca say they had some kind of charity luncheon today?' he asked. 'And Dani was going to go straight to Kristy's and stay there until after dinner.'

'Yeah,' Tyler said, staring at the gaping door. 'And your father's at work.'

Jason threw the car into park and killed the engine. He dashed to the door, Tyler right behind him.

Books, CDs and DVDs lay all over the living-room floor. The coffee table had been knocked over. The glass in his mother's curio cabinet smashed. The ottoman flipped and the bottom slit open.

Someone had come in and searched the place. And Jason was sure he knew exactly what they had been looking for.

THIRTEEN

Jason whipped around, grabbed Tyler by the shoulders and slammed him against the wall. 'Tell me again that you didn't steal an antique chalice from the Lafrenières!'

Tyler didn't look pissed off anymore. His face was pale, his pupils wide. 'I didn't know they'd do anything like this. If I'd thought it would somehow come back to your family . . .'

But it *had* come back to Jason's family. Tyler brought the vampires right into Jason's home. What would have happened if his parents or his aunt or Dani had been here? The thought made his body go hot, then cold.

'So you took it. Just admit it,' Jason ordered.

Tyler twisted away from him. 'I had no choice.'

'Bull.'

'You're right.' Tyler strode into the living room and began picking up books and shoving them back on the bookshelf. 'I had a choice. I could have let Russ kill me. You saw the bruises – that was just a taster.'

Jason followed Tyler, catching sight of the kitchen through the open door. The canisters of sugar, flour, and coffee had been dumped. The floor looked like some kind of toxic beach.

'Who's Russ?' he asked, joining Tyler in gathering up the books. He almost didn't want to know the answer.

'My dealer.'

'And? Come on, do I have to yank the whole story out of you word by word?'

'I stole from him, all right? I needed some Ritalin. I got addicted to the stuff. I didn't have the cash. Russ wouldn't front me, so I took it. A lot of it,' Tyler confessed. 'Like five thousand dollars worth.'

'Christ.' Jason let out a long breath.

'On a tricycle with a monkey on his back,' Tyler added, without a trace of humor in his voice.

'That call I answered? That was—?'

'That was Russ. He's my new best friend. Calls all the time,' Tyler said. 'Thanks for telling him where I was, by the way.' He jammed a book onto a shelf hard enough to make the case shake.

'I'm not used to my friends being chased by people who want them dead,' Jason countered. He moved toward another book and heard a sharp crack. He pulled his foot back. 'Great! You now owe my mother a *Celine Dion's Greatest Hits* CD.' He glanced around the room. 'Among other things,' he added under his breath.

'Look, Russ gave me forty-eight hours to get him cash for what I stole,' Tyler said. 'And I wasn't kidding about him sending somebody out here to kill me. Or at least seriously mess me up. I figured the Lafrenières have insurance up the wazoo. I thought they'd just submit a claim. No harm. No foul.'

Tyler lifted his arms, then let them fall to his sides. 'How was I supposed to know they'd do something like this? You saw their house. They have more crap than they could use in five lives. Why would they care so much?'

'You picked the wrong thing to steal,' Jason told him. 'That chalice has been in their family for generations. That's why they care so much.' A thought struck him like a knife in the chest. 'Was it even here when they trashed the place?'

Tyler shook his head. 'I sold it at a pawn shop.'

'Then this isn't over. They aren't going to stop until they get it back. And, obviously' – Jason kicked the overturned ottoman – 'they know you're the one who took the thing. We've got to go get it.'

'With what? I wired the money to Michigan already. I have . . .' Tyler pulled his wallet out of his back pocket and checked the contents, 'fifty-four dollars total.'

'We'll figure that out later. We've got to get to the pawn shop before they sell it,' Jason said. 'Because somebody else might be looking to mess you up if we don't.' He hesitated. 'It'll only slow us down if I call Dad now and try to tell him some version of what happened. So let's hit it,' he told Tyler. His mind was racing. If only Tyler had told him the whole story before, maybe he could have done something . . . Maybe he could get him out of the mess now, lend him the money somehow?

'I'm surprised you actually managed to find a pawn shop in Malibu,' Jason said as Tyler pushed the buzzer next to the door.

'Rich people probably need quick cash for their dealers every once in a while,' Tyler said. 'You can spend as much money as you have on drugs. More.'

Another buzz sounded. Tyler grabbed the doorknob and pulled the door open. Jason followed him inside. One wall held TVs, DVD players, CD players, and computers. A selection of cameras hung from the ceiling. Glass counters held an assortment of jewelry, including a variety of diamond engagement rings. It was pretty pathetic.

'Back already?' the middle-aged guy behind the counter asked Tyler. 'Got some more good stuff for me?' He gave his short, graying ponytail a tug.

'We need the gold chalice he sold you back,' Jason said.

'Not possible,' Ponytail Man answered. 'That thing flew out of here. I only had it in the case for a couple of hours.'

'Who bought it?' Jason demanded.

'This is the kind of place where people like their privacy,' Ponytail Man replied flatly.

'It's important,' Tyler put in. 'I'm kind of in a bad position.'

The man shrugged. 'It's also the kind of place where people are in bad positions a lot. I stay out of that.'

'We only want to find the buyer so we can buy back the chalice. We'll pay more than they paid. A lot more.' Jason had no idea where he or Tyler would come up with the money. A loan from Aunt Bianca, maybe? It didn't matter. For now, all he cared about was finding the chalice.

'Doesn't interest me,' Ponytail Man said. 'I don't give out buyer information.'

Jason shoved his fingers through his hair. 'How about this? How about if you contact the buyer for us? Tell them that we'll give them a profit if they'll sell us the chalice back.'

The man pulled a rag out of his back pocket and started to polish the closest counter. 'Of course, you'd get a percentage if the buyer agrees to sell,' Jason added quickly.

'Give me your phone number.' Ponytail Man slid a business card across the counter to Jason.

Jason carefully printed his cell number on the card and slid it back to the man. 'We really appreciate this.'

Ponytail Man grinned. 'I'll call you if they're interested.'

Jason waited. But it was clear the guy wasn't going to make the call while they were standing there, so he turned and led the way out of the place.

'Thanks for doing that,' Tyler told him as they walked down the sidewalk toward the car. 'I shouldn't have come here. I shouldn't have brought my crap into your life. Your parents have always been so great to me, and—'

'Enough, already,' Jason interrupted. 'You completely pissed me off. You lied to me. You got my house trashed. I may have to bust my college fund to save your ass. But you're my oldest friend. Who else were you supposed to come to?'

'There was no one else,' Tyler admitted.

'What do you think—?' Jason began.

An SUV with tinted windows pulled up alongside them and stopped. The side door slid open, fast and soundless. Immediately, two men leaped out, and Jason saw a flash of metal in the sunlight as a piece of pipe came down on Tyler's head.

Jason launched himself at the closest assailant. Another man moved in from the left and blocked him. Before Jason could make another attempt to reach Tyler, the men had him in the van and the door was sliding shut.

A second later the guy who'd blocked Jason was behind the wheel. Jason heard the van pull away. He stared after it. No license plate.

It sped around the corner and was gone. With Tyler inside.

FOURTEEN

Jason stared down the empty street. Adrenalin rushed through his body. Where were they taking Tyler? And what were they going to do to him when they got there?

His cell phone started to play *It's a Small World*, courtesy of Dani again. Jason jerked the cell out of his pocket and hit 'Talk'. 'Tyler?' he asked, knowing even as he said it that there was no possible way it was his friend.

'No, it's me. Sienna.'

Sienna. The last person he'd expected. Jason hadn't thought she'd ever want to talk to him again.

'You have to get Tyler out of Malibu. Right now,' she told him, her voice tight with tension.

'Too late.' Jason looked down the street again, as if somehow, magically, the SUV would come speeding backward toward him and the whole abduction would happen in reverse, leaving Tyler standing next to him.

'Two guys just snatched him. I was right there, but I couldn't stop it.'

Sienna didn't respond. But he could hear her breathing. 'I know where he is,' she said finally.

'Where? Tell me.'

She hesitated.

Come on, come on, come on! Jason urged silently. He didn't have time for this. *Tyler* didn't have time.

'Meet me at Zach's. At the gazebo in the side garden,' Sienna instructed.

'I'm on my way.' Jason started toward his car.

'And, Jason? Don't park where anyone can see you,' Sienna finished. She hung up before he could respond.

Jason parked a block away from Zach's. He cut down to the beach, figuring there was less chance of him being spotted if he approached the house from that way, rather than from the front. Although it occurred to him that all those decks and balconies would give anyone who happened to be looking a perfect view of him. He just had to hope no one had picked this moment to enjoy the ocean views.

He ran along the sand, his feet sinking into it with every step. Jason usually loved running on the beach, but right now he wanted some nice hard asphalt. A surface that would let him get some *speed*.

Sneakers wouldn't hurt either, he thought as he veered toward the rough wooden logs that served as stairs up the side of the cliff. A layer of sand had got between his Tevas and his feet.

Jason pounded up the steps and and raced over to the gazebo. Sienna was already waiting, her long, inky hair fluttering in the breeze coming off the ocean.

'Thanks for calling me,' he said when he reached her. 'So what gives?'

'Zach asked me to call,' Sienna told him. 'He thinks he owes you for saving his life in that fight with Luke Archer,' she continued. 'Zach doesn't like to owe anybody.'

'He doesn't owe me. He saved my life, too. But right now I'm not going to turn down his help,' Jason answered. 'Where's Tyler?'

'Zach wanted you to get him out of town.' Sienna twisted her hair into a knot to keep it from blowing in her face. 'But I really don't know what you can do now that it's too late for that.'

'Just tell me where he is and let me worry about the rest,' Jason said impatiently.

Sienna gave a reluctant nod. 'He's been taken before the Council.'

Questions exploded in Jason's head. 'The what?'

'The DeVere Heights Vampire Council,' Sienna repeated. 'It's this group that makes decisions about things that involve all of . . . of us.'

'Why would this council care about Tyler?' Jason demanded. 'Is it like steal from one of you and you steal from all of you?'

'What Tyler took was something that belonged to all of us, in a way,' Sienna explained. 'The Lafrenières keep the chalice because they are one of the oldest vampire families, but it doesn't truly belong to them. It's a sacred relic that has been used in our ceremonies for centuries.'

Nice one, Tyler, Jason thought. *The Lafrenière house is stuffed with expensive crap. And you had to grab some precious vampire artifact!*

'So what are they going to do with him?' Jason paced around the gazebo. He couldn't stand still. 'He's already sold the thing, but we have a lead on getting it back. We just need a little time.'

'I don't know,' Sienna admitted, her eyes even darker than usual – dark with apprehension. 'That's what they're deciding right now. But it doesn't look good. That's why Zach wanted you to get Tyler out of town before they found him.'

'Where is Zach?' Jason demanded. He and Jason weren't friends. Jason didn't know if Zach was actually friends with anyone – even any of the vampires. But Zach had power and, rightly or wrongly, he felt indebted to Jason. Right now, Jason could use that.

'He's at the meeting,' Sienna replied. 'He's on the Council now. That's why the chalice was out of the bank vault in the first place. It was used in the ceremony to inaugurate Zach onto the Council, the night of the party. The party was just to hide the fact that all the vampires were gathered. There was even a member of the High Council at the house that night.'

So that's why there was extra Zach-adoration at the party, Jason thought. 'OK, well, where does the Council meet?' he asked. His mind was racing. Maybe he could talk to the 'Council'. Explain that he had already been to the pawnbroker. That no matter what, he and Tyler would get the chalice back.

Or was it too late for talk?

'If I tell you that . . .' Sienna let her words trail off. She pulled her thin sweater tighter around herself.

'I get it. The Council could come after you,' Jason filled in for her. 'Look, I won't tell them who I got the information from. Just tell me where they are.'

'I don't care about me,' Sienna burst out, her voice

ragged with emotion. 'But if you try to interfere with the Council, they could kill you. I can't let that happen, Jason. It might be too late for you to save Tyler. But it's not too late for *me* to save *you*!'

Her words were so unexpected that Jason felt them like a punch to the gut. After all that had happened, he was amazed that Sienna actually cared. In the midst of the current crisis, part of him still found time to be ridiculously pleased that she did. But it didn't change anything. He reached out and touched her arm. 'Sienna, he's my best friend. I can't just . . .' He shook his head. 'I can't.'

'In the Garden,' she said simply.

Jason's eyes darted around the gardens surrounding the gazebo.

'No, up there.' Sienna pointed to the roof of the Lafrenière house. Sunlight glinted off huge panels of glass.

Jason frowned. He'd been on the top floor – all over the top floor – with Adam, and yet he hadn't seen those massive skylights. And, even at night, all that glass would have been impossible to miss.

And then suddenly, he got it. He and Adam hadn't *actually* been on the top floor at all. There was a whole other floor in the house. That's why he and Adam had seen the vampires go upstairs, but hadn't seen anyone there when they went up themselves.

'Go home, Sienna,' Jason said, his eyes fixed on the roof.

'What are you going to do?' she asked anxiously.

He turned to look at her, and couldn't resist running one finger down her soft, pale cheek. 'Don't worry about me. Just go.'

FIFTEEN

It's not like I can just go ring the doorbell and ask if I can please have my friend back, Jason thought, staring at the Lafrenière house. He pulled out his cell and punched in Adam's number. He had the strong, unpleasant feeling that he might need someone to get his back. Soon.

'Talk to me,' Adam said.

'I don't have time to explain, but I need you over at Zach's,' Jason told him. 'I'll be . . . I should be on the roof. North side.'

'Why would you—?' Adam began.

Jason hung up and surveyed the roof. Even a few more seconds could be critical to Tyler. But, since he wasn't freakin' Spiderman, how was he going to get up there to find out what was going on? Could the ivy and honeysuckle growing up the side of the house be strong enough to hold him? Jason trotted over to investigate.

Not a great option, he decided as he gave the thick

intertwined vines an experimental tug. But the only one that seemed to be available. And, hey, Sienna had climbed up a trellis in his dream, so this had to work. 'Here goes nothing,' Jason muttered, and reached up to grab a handful of the vines.

He slowly scaled the wall of the house, inch by inch. Leaves tore off in his fingers, but the thin vines held. For now. He moved up one story. Then another.

He ignored the sweat forming on his palms and between his toes. He tried to keep his movements even, putting steady pressure on the vines without jerking.

Snap!

The hunk of ivy and honeysuckle in Jason's right hand broke free. His body slipped, his feet sliding off the wall. His full weight now hung on the vines in his left hand. And he could feel them beginning to give . . .

One of the smaller balconies was just a little way above him and a few feet to the left. Jason swung out just as the vines tore. With one hand, he grabbed the balcony railing. The metal bit into his palm, and the muscles in his arm burned, but he slowly hauled himself up and over the railing.

Jason allowed himself to take a couple of deep breaths, then leaned over the railing to survey the damage. There were no longer any vines in reach above him. Unless . . .

He braced one hand against the wall and got himself balanced on top of the thin wrought-iron railing of the balcony. Then he twisted his body – and jumped. He managed to grab some of the vines high up above him in each hand. His feet scrambled against the stone wall, then found purchase. He scaled the rest of the wall as quickly as possible, trying to keep his weight on each section of vine for as short a time as possible.

And at last his fingers hit roof. Sweet, sweet roof. Jason pulled himself up onto it. One of the huge glass panes was about five feet away. He crawled over, and what he saw literally took his breath away.

Sienna had called the meeting place 'the Garden'. Jason had been expecting some sort of conservatory: lots of potted plants under glass. What he actually found was astounding.

Almost thirty feet below Jason, inside the house, smooth, green grass lawns stretched across the entire top floor of the Lafrenière mansion. Trees reached toward the windows, their top branches nearly brushing the glass. Birds of paradise, hibiscus, and other exotic-looking flowers Jason didn't know the names of blossomed everywhere. And a waterfall at the far end of the Garden splashed into a stream that meandered through the man-made glen. It looked like some kind of Eden. Extreme.

Through a cluster of trees, Jason spotted flashes of color. *People*, he thought. Well, vampires. The trees blocked most of his view. He'd have to move to a different window. Cautiously, attempting soundlessness, Jason crept across the roof toward the next of the enormous skylights.

A mosaic of black and white stone dominated this side of the Garden. A huge glass table stood on top of it. And standing around the table was a collection of Beautiful People. Capital B, capital P. *Make that a V*, Jason told himself. They were all vampires. But they looked like movie stars playing big-business execs. Power suits on the men. Dresses and skyscraper heels on most of the women, in colors that rivaled the flowers. Five-hundred-dollar haircuts all around. Manicures, of course. The undead knew how to take care of themselves.

Zach was the exception. Not that he wasn't a B.V. Jason had heard Dani rave about his intense dark brown eyes and his black hair and his perfect body. But Zach hadn't gone with a suit. Although Jason was pretty sure – thanks to Dani's fashion obsession – that his jeans were Armani. He couldn't make a call on the black T-shirt, though. It could have been out of some three-pack from the drug store. Could have been . . .

As if they'd been given a signal, all the vampires sat down. And Jason felt a rush of adrenalin.

Tyler sat in one of the chairs. No, 'sat' was the wrong word. He was slumped in one of the chairs, his head hanging so that his chin rested against his chest. Motionless.

For a horrible moment, Jason wondered if he was too late. Was Tyler already dead?

SIXTEEN

Jason stared at his friend. He was too far away to see if Tyler's chest was rising and falling. But, after a moment, he was sure he saw Tyler's hand twitch. Tyler was alive – apparently unconscious, but alive. The moron!

No, I'm *the moron! I never should have brought him to Zach's party*, Jason thought. *I shouldn't have let him get within a hundred yards of any of the vampires.*

But Jason knew that was not what he should be obsessing about now. He needed a plan to get Tyler away from the vampires. And he realized it would help him make *his* plan, if he knew what the vampires' plan was. Jason leaned closer to the glass in an effort to overhear the vampires' discussion below. He could hear nothing, but he felt something hard pressing into his chest.

Jason twisted around and slid sideways so that he could see what it was. He found that he was lying on a latch. The massive skylight actually opened.

Could he risk it? The ceiling of the Garden was tall – tall enough to allow for full-sized trees. Jason decided he could probably ease the window open without attracting the vampires' attention. He flipped the latch and gradually inched the window up. Thankfully, the skylight glided open smoothly and soundlessly. The scent of eucalyptus, bay, and grass filled the air.

Jason scanned the vampires at the table below him. Not one of them glanced up. He could see a guy in a charcoal suit talking. But he still couldn't hear what he was saying. Crap. He had to get closer.

Jason chose the thickest branch on the closest eucalyptus tree, which stood about thirty feet from the Council table. Without giving himself time to think, he slithered forward on his belly and leaned down until he could reach the branch, then he grabbed hold and swung himself into the air. *Another branch, another branch. I need another branch*, Jason thought, feeling around frantically with his feet. Luckily, he was now screened by the sharp-smelling eucalyptus leaves, but he could only cling to his branch for so long . . .

One of his toes hit something hard. OK. Jason carefully got both feet positioned on the branch below, then inched closer to the trunk. Now he could hear the man's voice, but not his actual words. He had to get closer still.

His heart pounded as he began to climb – agonizingly slowly – down the tree. He chose each step and handhold carefully, attempting complete silence.

Jason finally paused on a branch about fifteen feet above the ground. At first all he could hear was his pulse thumping in his ears. But the sound faded as his heart returned to its normal rhythm, and he found he could make out what the man was saying. He wriggled around until he could see Charcoal Suit through the leaves and branches. All eyes were on him as he spoke. No one glanced in Jason's direction.

'. . . pawnbroker sold it,' Charcoal Suit continued. 'The boy doesn't have anything to tell us. He's useless.'

So let him go, Jason urged silently.

'So let's dump him before he regains consciousness,' Zach said, echoing Jason's thought. 'He doesn't know anything. He can't connect us to anything that's happened to him.'

Jason suspected Zach was more interested in making the score even between himself and Jason than in Tyler's well being. But Jason would take that for now. *Good thing the guy hates to owe anyone*, he thought.

'That's only part of the issue,' a woman with a blond bun responded. 'He stole from all of us.'

'So turn him over to the cops along with the security tape. Stealing from the Lafrenières will be treated seriously by our loyal men in blue,' Zach said with a grin, sticking one foot up on the glass table.

Blond Bun stared at his top-of-the-line hiking boot in disgust, but she didn't comment.

'How many tickets did we buy to the Policemen's Ball, Dad?' Zach asked the man sitting across the table from him. Jason noted that Zach's father had the same black hair as Zach, but his eyes were lighter, a silvery grey.

'A more than adequate amount,' Mr Lafrenière answered. He stared pointedly at Zach's foot on the table. Zach didn't move it. 'I'm sure they would be happy to make things very unpleasant for the young man,' he added, indicating Tyler with a nod of his head.

Unpleasant was . . . unpleasant, of course, but Jason could easily imagine much worse things. He prayed that Zach and his father would convince the rest of the Council.

'Unpleasant isn't good enough,' Blond Bun insisted. 'There are people out there who know the history of the chalice. If it falls into the wrong hands, our whole community is threatened. He's endangered us all!' There were murmurs of agreement from what Jason estimated to be at least half of the Council.

'So we get it back,' Zach said with a shrug. 'That's the solution. We get it back and no one sees it.'

Right. No harm, no foul. Jason looked hopefully at the other vampires around the table, to see if they seemed to agree.

'Our newest member of the Council certainly is chatty,' put in a woman with a diamond on one finger that could choke a horse, frowning at Zach.

Zach ignored her. 'We have the resources to find the buyer.' Zach raised one dark eyebrow. 'Or am I wrong?' His tone made it clear he was sure that wasn't a possibility.

Everyone else at the table was older than Zach. But he had their full attention. Jason smiled – maybe Zach had the *cojones* to pull this off.

'You're right,' Charcoal Suit answered. 'And, of course, we'll do whatever we have to to get the chalice back. But that's a separate question. We're talking about what to do with the boy.'

'Kill him,' a man with collar-length red hair said calmly. Jason bit his lip.

'I agree.' Blond Bun gave a firm nod. 'We can't tolerate such a lack of respect.'

'But it's not as if he knows who we are,' a woman with blood-red lipstick told the group. Relief flooded through Jason, even though her lipstick was kind of freaking him out. 'It's not as though he decided to steal from us on purpose.'

'Does that matter?' Charcoal Suit asked.

'Not to me,' Red Hair answered. 'I don't care about motive. I care about action.'

'You care about vengeance,' Zach muttered.

Way to go, Zach! Jason murmured soundlessly.

'That's enough,' Mr Lafrenière barked at Zach. 'Being asked to join the Council is an honor. An honor that can be revoked!' He sighed. 'We all appreciate the way you dealt with Luke Archer, Zach,' he added more calmly. There were several nods around the table. 'But you were too impulsive. Too wild. You still have a lot to learn.'

Zach dropped his foot back to the ground. 'I killed Luke Archer because he stopped following our rules,' Zach said. 'We don't murder. Or has that changed?' He looked over at his father. So did everyone else.

The silence that filled the Garden felt as if it had physical weight. Jason found he was holding his breath.

At last Zach's father responded. 'We never feed to the point of death,' he said flatly.

'I understand the need to kill a vampire – or a human – who is a threat to us,' an older man with a mane of silvery hair said quietly. 'But I honestly don't see the danger in letting the boy live. I think we're sliding into the realms of revenge here.'

'I agree. I'm not at all comfortable killing him simply because he stole from one of us,' Freaky Lipstick added.

'All of us,' Horse-choking Diamond murmured.

'Murdering a thief is worse than what Archer did, because we'd be killing calmly and rationally,' Silver Hair said. 'Not in the grip of the bloodlust.'

'I don't see the point of more discussion,' Charcoal Suit cut in loudly. 'It's time for the vote.'

Mr Lafrenière nodded gravely and leaned forward. 'I second that.'

A vote on whether Tyler lived or died. Jason shook his head in an effort to dispel the horror that was threatening to cloud his brain. He scanned the enormous room, looking for all possible exits. If they voted to kill Tyler, he was going to have to move fast.

He listened to the voices as each member of the Council handed down a verdict. Six to six. A tie. Now what?

'Shouldn't the decision to kill be unanimous?' Freaky Lipstick asked.

'Good point!' Jason whispered.

'We've never required a unanimous vote before,' Blond Bun reminded her.

'Have you ever voted to slaughter a human before?' Zach asked lazily.

Jason saw Blond Bun stiffen at the word 'slaughter'. Good.

'Our visitor from the High Council will be here any minute and will cast the deciding vote,' Mr Lafrenière said firmly, before any of the others could respond.

'Of course,' Charcoal Suit agreed without hesitation, and there was an almost universal murmur of assent from the others around the table.

OK, now time for a bathroom break, Jason thought. *Or everybody downstairs for coffee and donuts. Whatever. Just leave long enough for me to get Tyler out of here.*

Nobody moved.

If the High Council member voted the wrong way, what was he going to do? The closest exit – the only exit Jason could see, other than the windows – was back by the waterfall. It was a certainty that he wouldn't be able to get Tyler over there without a fight – and he couldn't possibly fight all of them. Would they kill Tyler as soon as the deciding vote was cast? Jason wondered. Or was there some kind of ceremony that might buy him some time?

Jason saw one half of the large double doors by the waterfall swing open. He couldn't see who had entered – his view was blocked by the branches – but all the vampires fell silent. Now there was only the sound of rushing water and the faint rustle of leaves.

Mr Lafrenière moved out of Jason's line of sight. A moment later, he returned with a woman. Jason could see the top of her head – dark hair in a ponytail – but that was it. Zach's father was blocking her.

A woman, Jason thought, surprised. Well, why not? Just because there'd never been a woman president didn't mean the vampires weren't more enlightened. Cautiously, he parted the closest branches trying to get a better look. Was she someone he knew? The mother of someone he went to school with? Or was she from France? Maybe all the High Council members came from the homeland.

He still couldn't see her face, and he was afraid that if he pressed on the branches any harder, one of them would snap. And then Tyler wouldn't be the only one in need of a rescue mission.

'Madame High Councilor, please take my chair,' Mr Lafrenière said. 'We've found ourselves at a stalemate. We need you to cast the final vote.'

'Of course,' the High Councilor answered, her voice low and gravelly. And somehow familiar.

She sat down, and at last Jason could see her face. He almost fell out of the eucalyptus tree in shock.

He was looking at his Aunt Bianca.

SEVENTEEN

Bianca was a vampire.

Jason stared at her, for some reason remembering the toy bulldozer she'd given him for his fifth birthday, and how she'd sat in the backyard with him for hours, using it to make a road. He remembered her visiting him in the hospital when he was eleven and had his tonsils out. She'd taught him how to play poker that day. He remembered her taking him to the best concert of his life in Madison Square Garden when he was fifteen.

And then he remembered her coming out of the pool house on Thanksgiving, leaving Joe the pool guy in there practically walking into walls and giggling. *She fed on him*, Jason realized grimly. *Right there in our pool house.*

Jason's mind was reeling with shock and confusion. How could Aunt Bianca – the person of whom he had so many good memories – be a vampire? How could his *mother's sister* be a vampire?

His mother's sister. A trickle of cold sweat ran down Jason's back. Aunt Bianca and his mother both had blue eyes and incredibly slim ankles. And they both had that weird thing where their second toe was longer than their big toe. Did that mean . . . ? Could that mean his mother was a vampire too? Sienna had told him vampirism was hereditary.

But . . . his *mother*? That would mean he and Dani would have to be at least half—

Jason realized his aunt had begun to speak. He shoved all his questions aside and tried to focus.

'This isn't something I want to do,' she was saying, her voice cool and crisp and oh, so businesslike. 'But our safety has been compromised by the theft of the chalice. We can't allow that to happen. We have to show anyone who may be watching that we will do whatever is necessary to protect ourselves.'

Bianca stared calmly at Tyler. 'I vote that the boy should die.'

And at that moment, Jason mentally disowned his aunt. She knew Tyler. She'd known him since Jason was a little kid. She'd had breakfast with him that morning. And now she was calmly commanding his death.

Jason frowned, his mind focused and racing now.

He was determined to find a way to rescue Tyler. But there were thirteen vampires down there. Jason smiled grimly – he didn't fancy his odds.

'I'll dispose of him. Not here, of course,' Bianca was saying briskly. 'Zach, help me get him down to my car. I think he's about to regain consciousness and the less he sees of this place – and any of you – the better.'

Jason saw a glimmer of hope. His aunt and Zach – he felt more confident about taking on the two of them. Sure, they were both vampires with super-human strength, but he had some fighting skills – and maybe Zach would still be feeling indebted.

Jason's cell phone rang. His body jerked, and for the second time he almost fell off his branch. He yanked the cell out of his pocket and managed to turn it off two notes into *It's a Small World*.

He scanned the faces of the vampires. A few of them were glancing around the table as if they'd heard the sound. But no one was looking up. Jason checked the number of the incoming call. Adam. He texted a quick message: 'Wait. Quiet.'

Bianca and Zach were half-carrying, half-dragging Tyler toward the door by the waterfall now. Jason needed to get out of the Garden and formulate a plan.

'The rest of you leave a few at a time,' Bianca ordered over her shoulder as Jason started back up the tree.

The leaves trembled as he moved from branch to branch. All he could do was pray his luck held. And it seemed to. No one shouted out as he grabbed the edge of the skylight and scrambled back onto the roof. Gently, he slid the glass pane closed.

Now he just had to get himself to the ground – easy, except that a chunk of his vine ladder was now missing. Jason stretched out on his belly and surveyed the side of the house. To his horror he saw that more than a chunk had gone – the honeysuckle and ivy had crumpled to the ground from the spot where they tore. There was no getting down that way.

Luckily, Jason had another idea. He inched down the section of vines that remained, then grabbed the railing of the balcony he'd used before. Now came the tricky part. There was another balcony below this one, but it was off to the right.

Jason swung out and back, building up momentum. One. Two. Three. He released the railing, letting himself fly backward through the air. He landed on the floor of the lower balcony, hard enough to knock the breath out of him for a moment.

'Are you insane?' Adam called up to him when Jason got back on his feet.

Jason signaled frantically for him to shut up, then climbed over the balcony rail and used the railing to lower himself as far as he could. He checked the bushes below him. They should help. A little, he thought. Then he let go.

'I don't need an answer,' Adam said as he rushed over and helped Jason out of the thick, prickly brush. 'I can already see you are certifiable.'

'I feel like I am,' Jason told him. 'I just found out my Aunt Bianca is a vampire. And not just any vampire. She's on something they call the "High Council".'

'Why do I think that's not the group in charge of Vampire Bingo?' Adam asked.

'She was meeting with the DeVere Heights Council to decide what to do with Tyler. Short version – at Zach's party, he stole a priceless artifact the vampires use in their ceremonies. And the Council just voted to kill him for it. Aunt Bianca's going to do it. She's going to take him . . . wherever, and just off him.'

'Wait. Your aunt is a vampire?' Adam repeated. Jason wasn't sure whether he'd actually taken in anything else. 'What does that mean about your mom? And, not to get too personal, you? The whole thing is supposed to be inherited, right?'

'I thought of that.' Reflexively, Jason ran his tongue over his teeth. Pretty blunt. 'I'm not. I can't be. I'd have to know, wouldn't I?'

'You haven't been drinking any blood lately, have you?'

'No,' Jason answered quickly. 'Well, if I cut my finger or something I lick it. Is that weird?' Suddenly, the taste flooded his mouth: salty, metallic, warm. He felt his gag reflex kick in. Surely that was a good sign.

'Everybody does that,' Adam told him. 'Does your mom know about your aunt, do you think?'

'I'm not sure,' Jason admitted. 'It shocked the hell out of me. And there's no way Dani would know if I don't. If my mom does know what Bianca is, she's keeping it a big secret. I guess it's possible, but I seriously doubt—'

Jason stopped. He could feel the outline of a plan forming. 'I'm not supposed to know about Aunt Bianca,' he muttered.

'Yeah. That's kind of the definition of a secret,' Adam said. 'Did you hit that soft spot on your head when you fell?'

'But, listen, we can use the secret thing. Bianca isn't going to want to say or do anything in front of me that would make me realize she isn't just my regular, *human* aunt,' Jason explained. He pulled his keys out of his pocket and handed them to Adam. 'So, go get my car and bring it right up to the front door of the house, OK? I parked down the block.'

'I saw. I'm gone.' Adam sprinted away.

Jason positioned himself at the side of the house, in sight of Bianca's rented red Mustang convertible and the front door. Then waited. He mentally rehearsed what he was going to say, hoping that he'd be able to sound convincing. It's not like he was much of an actor. His last time on stage was as a potato in the third-grade play.

He ran his fingers through his hair, pulling out a leaf, and smoothed down his shirt. He needed to look normal when he talked to his aunt. Otherwise he'd blow the plan. *You're not going to blow it*, he told himself firmly. *Tyler's life depends on that!*

Where were Bianca and Zach? How long could it take them to get Tyler downstairs? Jason wondered. They hadn't decided to kill Zach in the house, had they? No, that didn't make sense. The mess for one thing. They wouldn't want to get blood all over the Lafrenière showplace. Unless they killed him in a bloodless way. Would they just drain him? Would they figure, why not use the blood for—?

The front door swung open, snapping Jason out of his thoughts. Bianca and Zach emerged, supporting Tyler between them. His eyes were open now, and he was walking. He'd clearly fall if they let him go, but he was at least able to move his legs. Jason let out a breath that he hadn't even realized he'd been holding.

'Zach! Tyler! Hey!' Jason called, strolling towards them all. His voice came out a little too loud. A little nervous-sounding, maybe. But passable. He hoped. 'Aunt Bianca! What are you doing here?' Jason decided he would be the one asking the questions. Let her play defense.

Her eyes widened, but she answered smoothly enough. 'I was dropping off a book for Zach's father,' she said quickly. 'Something I knew Stefan would want him to have.'

So you're a vampire and *a stellar liar*, Jason thought. *Way to go, Aunt Bianca!*

His aunt smiled. 'And, as you can see, I found our Tyler having a bit too much fun with Zach.'

'Tyler, man, you couldn't wait for me?' Jason asked.

'What?' Tyler mumbled.

'You know I'm always up for fun.' He tapped his friend's chest, wanting Tyler to know that he was there.

'Let's get him into my car, Zach,' Bianca said. 'He's

getting heavy.' She and Zach took a step toward the red Mustang.

Jason stepped in front of them, blocking their way. 'You'll be sorry if you put him in your car,' Jason warned. 'I know Tyler. I know his pre-puke face. And this is it. He'll ruin your upholstery. I'll drive him home.'

'In what?' Bianca asked. 'I don't see your car.'

Zach didn't speak, but his eyes moved back and forth between Jason and Bianca like he was watching a tennis match.

'Adam's on his way over with it. I asked him to drive. I wanted to take a run on the beach,' Jason explained, the trickle of sweat beginning to run down his back again. He could feel it starting to glue his shirt to his skin. 'He'll be here in a sec.'

'I'm not sure Tyler can stand up another sec,' Bianca said, taking a step forward and forcing Tyler – and Zach – with her. Jason had to back up a little. 'Don't worry about my car. It's a rental,' she added cheerfully.

Tyler's knees buckled. Zach and Bianca had to tighten their grip on him to keep him on his feet. Jason took advantage of the situation. 'I got him,' he said, grabbing Tyler's arm.

Bianca rushed over to the Mustang and opened the

passenger door. 'You can trust me to take Tyler home and tuck him into bed,' she said sweetly. 'Let's get him sitting down.'

Phenomenal liar, Jason thought. *Pure ice.*

'That would humiliate him,' Jason said. 'He, uh, he has a crush on you.' He turned to Zach, desperately playing for time. 'You can see why he'd have a crush on my aunt, right?'

Zach ran his eyes from Bianca's silky dark hair to her black spike heels. 'Absolutely,' he announced calmly.

'Absolutely,' Jason repeated. Now sweat was popping out on his forehead. Would Bianca notice? Would it make her suspicious? *Don't think about it. Keep talking*, he ordered himself. 'Absolutely,' he said again. 'And Tyler wouldn't want the woman he's hot for – sorry, Aunt Bianca, I mean attracted to – tucking him into bed.'

'Unless she was with him,' Zach added.

'Right. So you should let me take care of Tyler,' Jason urged. And then he heard a wonderful, miraculous sound. He glanced over his shoulder. Yeah. It was the Bug. 'And Adam's here with the car now, so, *no problemo*. We'll cart Tyler home.'

Adam pulled up right next to Bianca's car. He jumped out and opened the passenger door. Jason hustled Tyler into the passenger seat, then slid behind the wheel. Adam jumped into the tiny backseat.

This is it, Jason thought. He knew his aunt had very few choices left. Either she had to give up the kindly aunt pretense and out herself as a vampire. Or she had to let them leave.

Which was it going to be?

EIGHTEEN

'See you back at the house,' Bianca said, her blue eyes ice-cold.

Jason realized with a huge rush of relief that his gamble had paid off. Bianca wasn't willing to reveal the truth about herself. At least, not yet.

He smiled at her, nodded and put his foot on the gas.

'Where are we?' Tyler mumbled.

'We are now leaving hell,' Jason told him as they sped through the massive iron gates that guarded the Lafrenière property.

'OK,' Tyler said, head lolling.

Jason pulled up next to Adam's Vespa and stopped. 'Thanks. I didn't have anyone else to call.'

Adam nodded. 'Are you going to be OK from here?' he asked. 'I'm available for more sidekick duty – as long as I don't have to start wearing yellow tights or anything.'

'I'm good. And no one with the middle name Tecumseh can be a sidekick,' Jason replied. He needed to find a place to stash Tyler. And he knew it could put Adam in danger – more danger than he was already in – if he knew where that place was.

'Call me later and tell me how it goes, Batman,' Adam joked. But his eyes were serious.

Jason nodded, then started to drive out of DeVere Heights as the twilight deepened to night. His cell rang. A number he didn't recognize. He answered it. 'Yeah.'

'Take Tyler straight to the airport,' a low, cool voice said. It took Jason half a second to recognize it: Zach. 'Sienna will meet you there with cash. Terminal 3.'

'Got it.' Jason glanced over at Tyler. The cool breeze seemed to be reviving him a little. 'And thanks.'

'We're even now, Freeman,' Zach replied. 'Don't expect any more favors.' And then the line went dead.

Jason didn't care. The favor Zach had already done him was probably going to save Tyler's life. And Jason very much hoped he'd never need another favor from Zach, ever.

He pulled out onto the Pacific Coast Highway for what felt like the hundredth time that day. PCH had a completely different vibe at night. Eerie. The ocean stretched away down below the road, a dark, endless abyss.

Jason saw headlights appear in his rear-view mirror. Someone was coming up fast behind him. But who? The car flashed its brights, blinding him for a moment. Was it Bianca? One of the other vampires from the Council? The hit squad that had picked up Tyler in the SUV?

This was a bad place to be followed. The empty beach ran for miles on one side. And now that they were outside of Malibu, there were very few exits on the other. Jason figured he could veer off into one of the little beach towns, and try to lose whoever was behind him in the warren of little streets. But he didn't know the area. He could end up turning down a dead end – and somebody could end up dead.

Jason checked the rear-view again. The car moved into the left lane and drew up alongside. He could see it now: a Mustang – red, like Bianca's.

'Tyler, stay low,' Jason ordered.

'What's going on?' Tyler asked, frowning at him. His eyes were clearer now.

'Later,' Jason told him.

The driver honked and flashed the brights again. Were they trying to get him to pull over? And then what? Just hand Tyler over to them? Jason's fingers tightened on the wheel as he tried to decide how to play it.

He could floor it – but he wasn't sure the Bug could outrun the Mustang. He could slam into the other car and maybe it would knock the driver – Bianca? – out. Those seemed like his only options.

The Mustang picked up speed until it was level with Jason. He didn't recognize the driver.

He *didn't* recognize the driver!

It *wasn't* one of the vampires from the Council. It *definitely* wasn't his aunt. It was some middle-aged guy with gray hair, wearing a leather jacket and a goofy Red Baron-type silk scarf. That plus the red Mustang convertible equaled mid-life crisis. Jason let out a sigh of relief.

'One of your tail lights is out,' the Red Baron yelled. 'You're going to get pulled over.' Jason waved his thanks, and the Baron accelerated around him with a cheerful *toot-toot*.

Jason immediately checked behind him. Only blackness. Unless someone was back there driving with the headlights off, he and Tyler were safe. For now.

'Can you answer my question now?' Tyler's voice had lost the muzzy quality.

'What do you remember?' Jason asked, stalling.

'I remember us going to the pawn shop and that the guy had already sold the chalice,' Tyler answered. 'I remember . . . smelling flowers. And was I in Zach's house?'

'You've lost a little memory,' Jason told him, relieved that he had. It would make things easier.

'When we came out of the pawn shop, two guys jumped you. Knocked you out. You took a pretty good smack to the head with a piece of pipe,' he explained. 'That's why you're out of it. From what they said when they were beating the hell out of you, they were from that dealer in Michigan.'

Tyler touched the back of his head and winced, then he turned and studied Jason. 'You look pretty good. You take a seat, have some popcorn and watch the show?' he joked, sounding more like his old self with every word.

'Nah. I'm just not as big a wimp as you are. I know how to handle myself in a fight,' Jason answered, grinning. He glanced at Tyler, then checked the rearview. Still no one there. 'Right now, we need to get you out of town. Those guys seemed pretty Terminator. I think they'll be back. Any ideas on where you want to go?'

'With my fifty bucks?' Tyler asked, staring out at the dark waves crashing against the darker rocks.

'Fifty-four,' Jason corrected. 'But no worries. Sienna's meeting us at the airport with traveling money. You just have to pick your final destination.'

'Back to Michigan, I guess,' Tyler said, still looking out at the ocean. 'At least I have a place to crash there.' He gave a snort of laughter. 'My dad probably hasn't even realized I'm gone. Or if he has, he just figures I'll be back when I get hungry.'

Bleak. But Tyler couldn't stay out here even if Jason's parents would agree. 'Is Michigan going to be safe? With the dealer and everything?'

'He'll have got the money I wired by the time I get home. It'll be cool.' Tyler turned to face Jason. 'It'll be cool,' he repeated. Like if he said it enough times it would be true.

'Maybe I'll come out there and visit,' Jason said. 'Experience a few days without sunshine and maybe some—' He stopped, his attention caught by a pair of headlights behind him. *Get a grip*, he told himself. *A lot of people use PCH.*

'Some what?' Tyler asked.

'Uh—' Jason kept his eyes on the headlights, trying to remember what he'd been about to say. He settled for, 'Some of that gray, slushy snow that gets down in your boots.'

'I can pretty much guarantee it.' Tyler looked over his shoulder. 'You don't think those are the guys back there, do you? Wanting to go another round?'

'Crossed my mind,' Jason admitted. 'But it's doubtful.' The car behind them hung back, keeping pace from a distance.

It *was* doubtful. But by now Bianca would have had time to get home. And she'd have realized that Jason hadn't returned with Tyler. What was she thinking? Was she coming to find them?

'Uh, I could use some caffeine,' Jason said. 'Maybe some barbeque potato chips. We can't be driving all the way to the airport without provisions.' He glanced at the car again. It was still back there. Taking a little detour would show whether he and Tyler were just being paranoid, or if they had something real to worry about.

'My treat,' Tyler answered, his eyes also on the rear-view mirror.

Jason turned off on Tuna Canyon Road. So did the car behind them.

'Maybe they're after caffeine too,' Tyler suggested, but he didn't sound like he believed it.

This is what Jason had wanted to avoid. Ending up in some kind of chase in an area he didn't know. He spotted the neon sign of a mini-mart up ahead. He'd only said he wanted to do a junk-food stop so they'd have an excuse to pull off the highway. But a mini-mart meant witnesses. And that felt like a very good thing right now.

He sped up and pulled into the parking lot. The car – a station wagon with wooden panels that had got the *Pimp My Ride* treatment – pulled in behind them. 'Let's get inside,' Jason urged.

He and Tyler scrambled out of the Bug and rushed into the store. An electronic bell announced their arrival. A moment later, it rang again. Jason looked toward the door. Two strangers had come in and were heading for the beer. Another false alarm. Man, he was going to be one of the few seventeen-year-olds to experience heart failure if he didn't get his paranoia in check.

Except, Jason reminded himself, *what was that T-shirt slogan? 'Just because you're paranoid doesn't mean they're not out to get you'*.

He loaded up on Mountain Dew – he felt like he'd been awake for about three days – then grabbed the biggest bag of BBQ Ruffles available. Dani would say he was stress-eating. But who cared?

Tyler paid up. Jason used the time to reprogram the

ring on his phone. Then they headed back to the Bug. And back to the highway.

The closer they got to L.A., the more traffic filled the road. Jason couldn't keep tabs on all the drivers. He knew they could be being followed right now, and not even know it. The number of cars would give cover to anyone tailing them.

'What's that up there?' Tyler asked.

'It's the Ferris wheel on the Santa Monica Pier,' Jason answered.

It was hard to believe that crowds of people were out on the pier, having fun under the colorful lights. Playing Skee-Ball. Eating junk food. Giving fake screams in the stupid haunted house. How could all that be going on when his friend had almost been murdered tonight?

His mind kept returning to the expression on his aunt's face when she gave the vote that meant Tyler's death. So calm. So rational.

'I know I'm the visitor, but shouldn't we be heading toward that exit?' Tyler asked.

Jason realized that he'd almost missed the ramp to the 405. He glanced over his shoulder, then cut over a couple of lanes, just reaching the exit in time. 'Good catch,' he told Tyler.

'Well, it said that way to the airport, and I thought since we were going to the airport . . .'

'It's not very far from here,' Jason said. He focused on the signage and managed to get them to LAX with only one U-turn, then into the big cement parking garage for Terminal 3.

Jason and Tyler left the Bug in the garage and cut across the bumper-to-bumper airport traffic to reach the terminal. Jason did a Sienna scan. There were lots of people around, but it wasn't as though she was easy to miss. She wasn't there yet.

'Let's check out the flights to Michigan.' He led the way over to the bank of Arrival/Departure monitors.

'There's one in a little less than an hour: Midwest Express,' Tyler said. 'Never heard of them, but, whatever.'

Jason did another Sienna check. This time he saw her. He waved, and she hurried toward them without smiling. All that emotion she'd shown when she tried to stop him from going after Tyler was gone.

'We found a flight,' Jason told her.

And, after that, everything happened very quickly. Tyler bought a ticket with the money Sienna gave him. He had to go directly to security for check-in, and they weren't allowed to go with him past the metal detectors.

'So, I guess I'll see you in Michigan sometime. Maybe,' Tyler said when he was two people away from the detectors.

'Yup, I'm coming. And I'm going to whip your butt in basketball,' Jason replied with a grin.

Tyler surprised him by grabbing him and hugging him hard. 'Thank you. I'm going to get it together. Let me know what I owe you, man. I'll get the money and pay you back. You can count on it,' he promised. Then he walked through the metal detector and disappeared from sight.

It was then that Jason realized Sienna was no longer standing next to him. He spun around and saw her striding toward the closest exit. 'Sienna! Wait!' he called. She didn't turn around. It was like what had happened between them in the gazebo had been erased from her memory.

Jason sprinted after her and grabbed her arm. 'I said wait!'

She whirled around to face him. 'Tyler's on his way to the plane. You don't need me anymore,' she snapped, trying to pull free. 'And in, oh, maybe another two seconds you'll be wanting to get away from me anyway, right? You obviously can't manage to feel the same way about me for more than two minutes at a time.'

Jason did the only thing he could think of. He kissed her. Fast, before she had time to react. Hard, because he had been wanting to for so long.

Everything fell away except the feel of her mouth on his. Complete inferno.

A passenger in a hurry let his heavy suitcase slam into their legs, and they stumbled apart. Sienna reached down and rubbed her calf.

Slowly, the world around Jason came into focus. There were people everywhere. All he wanted to do was kiss Sienna again. But this wasn't exactly the place. 'Let me walk you to your car,' he offered.

'OK.' She was back to not quite looking at him as they headed outside and crossed the street to the garage. 'I'm glad that Tyler's OK.' She paused. 'And you too.'

'It got a little hairy there for awhile. It would have gone a lot differently, a lot worse, without you and Zach. Thank you.'

'I'm on the second floor,' she answered.

He opened the door to the stairwell and let Sienna go in ahead of him. Maybe they could just camp out here on the cement steps. Never go back to the real world. He glanced at her, wishing she had a little screen running across her forehead that spelled out her thoughts.

'What?' she asked.

Jason realized he'd been staring. 'I was just wondering about my aunt, the High Council member,' he said. Because he couldn't tell Sienna what he'd been really thinking. And, anyway, he did wonder about his aunt.

'I should have told you about her. But she didn't want anyone in your family to know,' Sienna said. She opened the door to the second floor of the parking garage and they walked over to her Spider.

Jason hated watching her slide behind the wheel. They'd hardly had any time together. And who knew when they'd be alone again.

Sienna turned the key. The Spider gave a groan of protest. 'Not again!' Sienna cried.

Oh, yeah! The Spider came through for Jason. How much did he love that car? So very much. 'Guess you need a ride,' he said, feeling a grin spread across his face.

Sienna got out of the car and slammed the door. 'I guess I do.'

A half an hour later, Jason pulled back onto PCH, the lights from the Santa Monica Pier glittering in the darkness. And now it felt completely right that there were people out there having fun. Eating bad food.

Playing games. Pretending to be scared by plywood monsters. Making out on the sand under the boardwalk. Having Sienna with him changed everything.

'Tyler should be boarding his plane right around now,' Sienna said.

'Yeah. And by now my aunt must know for sure that he's gone.' Jason shook his head. 'I have no idea what to expect when I get home.'

'She'll probably act completely normal. Maybe a little worried because she expected you at home.' Sienna reached out and put her hand over his for a brief moment. 'She's not going to want the DeVere Heights Council or the other members of the High Council to know she let Tyler get away. So she won't tell anyone. And it's not like Zach or I will say anything. I think Tyler's pretty safe.'

'Can I ask you something else?' Jason went on without waiting for a yes. 'You said being a vampire is a hereditary thing. And Aunt Bianca's a vampire, right? So that should mean my mom is. And even Dani and me!'

Sienna laughed. 'Don't sweat it. You're not a vampire, neither is Dani, or your mom and dad.'

'So, how come? Bianca's adopted?'

'No. Well, not that I know of,' Sienna answered.

'Your aunt is more unusual than that – she's a human who chose to become a vampire.'

'That's possible?' Jason asked curiously. It hadn't occurred to him that there might be more ways than one of becoming a vampire.

'The only way a human can become one of us is if they bite back, if they drink the blood of a vampire as the vampire drinks from them,' Sienna explained. 'Usually, it doesn't ever happen because a vampire won't allow it. It's too much of a risk. When you're a born vampire, you grow up knowing that you have to protect yourself and your kind. You know how important it is to keep your nature a secret. But it's different for a turned vampire. They have so many ties to the human world. There's a much greater chance that they will put us in danger by trusting the wrong people.'

'I don't think Bianca has told my mom, and she usually tells my mom everything,' Jason said. 'But if *turned* vampires are sort of mistrusted, how did she get to be on the High Council? How'd she get to be a vampire at all?'

'Stefan loved her so much, that he was willing to risk everything for her!' Sienna said simply. 'If a vampire with any less power and prestige than Stefan had turned a human, the rest of the vampires would probably have banished him and your aunt. Or worse,' Sienna told him. 'But Stefan was descended from one of the very first families on the first High Council, formed back in the Renaissance. He was hugely respected, so Bianca was accepted. And when he died, Bianca inherited his spot on the High Council. She's more famous and powerful among vampires than anyone in DeVere Heights.' Sienna laughed. 'It's kind of like you're related to a rock star.'

'A rock star who can decide if someone lives or dies,' Jason replied grimly. 'It's going to be hard to walk into the house tonight and act like I don't know any of this.'

'But you have to,' Sienna told him, a little of the intensity that had been in her voice in the gazebo returning. 'I'm not sure you'll be safe if you don't.'

'I will. It'll be OK,' Jason reassured her as they drove through the massive gates leading into the Heights.

'It won't be OK until the chalice is returned,' Sienna said with a sigh. A breeze caught her long hair, blowing it across Jason's cheek. Bringing that mix of scents – green apple, and vanilla, and the ocean – that was pure Sienna.

'I'll do whatever I can to get it back,' Jason promised. He turned onto Sienna's street, then into her driveway. He turned off the engine, and the car fell quiet.

'So, well, goodnight,' Sienna said. But she didn't move, didn't reach for the door handle. She turned toward Jason.

He suddenly felt aware of every nerve ending. And of his pulse quickening as he looked into Sienna's eyes. He leaned toward her – until their lips met. And Jason knew that, in spite of Brad being his friend, in spite of Sienna being a vampire, he never wanted that moment to end.

And then his cell phone rang.

Sienna started to pull away, but Jason looped his hands in her hair, holding her close.

The phone continued to ring. Jason ignored it. He had been waiting for this kiss since the beginning of Thanksgiving vacation, which felt like a million years ago now.

He felt a jolt of adrenalin as Sienna's tongue brushed his. *It was definitely worth the wait*, he thought.

NINETEEN

Sienna gently eased away from him. 'I have to go in,' she whispered.

'OK,' Jason told her. 'But we have to figure all this out.' This meaning him, Sienna . . . and Brad. Jason's friend Brad. Sienna's boyfriend, Brad.

'We will. I promise. Just not tonight.' Sienna climbed out of the car and hurried up to her front door. He watched her until she had unlocked it. She turned and waved as she slipped inside.

Jason watched as the door closed, and imagined her heading into her bedroom. *Thinking about me?* he wondered as he started the car.

He checked his phone as he headed home. A voice-mail told him he had a message. He punched in his code and listened. The pawnbroker. He had the chalice. It hadn't been what the buyer wanted after all. Jason could have it back – but it would cost seven thousand dollars.

Seven *thousand* dollars. Might as well be seven million. *Where am I going to get that kind of money?* Jason wondered.

But a new worry shoved that thought aside when he pulled into his driveway. He could see a light on in the kitchen. Someone was waiting up for him.

Jason parked the car. As soon as he got inside the house he headed straight for the kitchen. *Might as well get this over with,* he told himself. As he had expected, his aunt sat at the table. The floor had been swept, the counters wiped down, everything was back in place.

'So there you are. Your parents were worried, what with the break-in and all. So was I,' Bianca said. 'I didn't tell them I had expected to see you here when I got back. That would have worried them even more.' She took a sip of coffee.

'Thanks.' Jason took a seat across from her.

'Where's Tyler? Passed out in the car?' Bianca asked. Her voice was relaxed, but there was a steely glint in her blue eyes. *She's dangerous,* Jason thought. *And not just because she's a vampire, but because there's something hard and cold and calculating inside her.* The realization was as sharp as a knife blade.

'I took him to Starbucks to pump some coffee into him after we left Zach's,' Jason explained, making sure to look his aunt in the eye. 'But he got a call from his dad when we were there. Got ordered home. I guess he didn't exactly have parental clearance to come out here.'

'Tyler went back to Michigan?' said a voice behind him.

Jason looked over his shoulder and saw Dani standing in the doorway, dressed in her monkey pajamas. 'Yeah. He needed to get home,' he told her. 'He said to tell you goodbye.'

'His father wouldn't even let him come back and get his things?' Bianca asked, and Jason could hear a note of suspicion in her voice.

'He didn't bring anything with him,' Jason explained quickly. 'He didn't really have permission to come visit in the first place.'

'Is he OK?' Dani joined them at the table. 'I'm worried about him.'

Bianca reached out and covered Dani's hand with her own. Watching his aunt with his sister put Jason on edge. *She'd never hurt Dani – or any of us*, he told himself firmly, trying to believe it.

'Tyler's always seemed like a boy who knows how to take care of himself,' Bianca told Dani. 'I'm sure he'll be fine.'

So she'd leave him alone? Was that what she was saying? There was no way to ask Bianca that without revealing that he knew the truth about her. *And that wouldn't be smart*, Jason thought as he headed upstairs for a few hours' sleep before school. *At all!*

Jason wrote out a check to cash for seven thousand dollars. His hand shook a little as he signed his name. His parents would implode when they found out he'd withdrawn a major chunk of his college fund.

No other choice, he told himself as he got in line for the cashier. No way was he taking more money from Zach. Jason had brought Tyler into the Lafrenière house. What had happened was his responsibility.

A bell dinged. Jason checked the lighted number on the monitor in front of him, then headed over to window three. He half expected the cashier to refuse to cash the check – even though he was at his own bank. But she just asked to see his driver's license, then had him sweep his ATM card through the machine and enter his PIN number.

Not much more than a minute later, he was walking back out into the afternoon sunshine with seven thousand dollars in cash in his pocket. He went directly to the pawn shop. Maybe there were people in the Heights who walked around with that kind of money on them routinely, but Jason just wanted to get rid of it.

The pawnbroker with the ponytail buzzed him inside with a wide smile. Why shouldn't he be smiling? He was about to make a two-thousand-dollar profit for doing nothing.

'Do you have the chalice?' Jason asked.

'If you got the money, I got the chalice,' Ponytail Man replied evenly.

'Plus more than a twenty-five per cent profit,' Jason muttered.

Ponytail Man shrugged. 'If it's too much, I'll keep the thing. I'm sure I can sell it again.'

They stared at each other. The man knew exactly how desperate Jason was. Jason had made that way clear when he was in the shop with Tyler. There was no point in trying to negotiate now. Jason pulled out the wad of cash and shoved it across the glass counter to the pawnbroker.

Ponytail Man counted it, fast and efficient. Then he reached under the cash register, pulled out a paper bag, and handed it to Jason. Jason peered inside. The chalice was there. It almost seemed to glow, even in the dim light of the shop. And it *pulled* at something in Jason. He wanted to take the chalice out of the bag and just hold it for a minute. But he closed the bag and hurried back out to his car. The chalice wasn't for him. The safest thing was to get rid of it as soon as possible.

Jason slid behind the wheel – and froze. A man was watching him from across the street. He tightened his grip on the chalice. Did the man know what was in the bag?

A truck rumbled down the street. It blocked the man from Jason's view for a few seconds. And when the truck had passed, the man was gone. Jason glanced up and down the street; there was nobody to be seen.

He fired up the Bug, telling himself that he was being paranoid, but the desire to get the chalice back where it belonged had just got stronger. So he didn't pass Go, didn't collect two hundred dollars. He drove straight to Zach's.

Zach met him in the driveway before Jason could reach the front door. 'I wasn't expecting to see you here again . . . so soon,' Zach said.

'Hello to you too.' Jason thrust the paper bag into Zach's hands. 'Something I think you'll be happy to see.'

Zach opened the bag, and raised one eyebrow. 'You keep coming through for us, Freeman.'

'*Now* we're even,' Jason told him.

Zach gave a reluctant smile.

'Don't expect any more favors,' Jason added, and Zach's smile widened into a grin.

Jason swung himself back into his Bug and headed for home. Things were back to normal.

As normal as they ever got in DeVere Heights.

MY
desperate LOVE
DIARY
by Liz Rettig

There's G. Isn't he gorgeous? I think he just looked at me – well, he looked in my direction anyway. Do you think he'd ask me out if I dyed my hair and got breast implants? KELLY ANN

*I think you need **brain** implants, Kelly Ann, then maybe you'd see what a complete idiot G is. STEPHANIE*

Stephanie's right. OK, G's not ugly but he's SO up himself! You'd be much better off with Chris. He's really fit and crazy about you, if only you'd open your eyes . . . LIZ

Don't be stupid! Chris is a good friend but that's it. I'd rather snog my brother (if I had one). Now be serious, how do I get G to notice me? A blonde wig and a Wonderbra? KELLY ANN

Navigating her way through teenage embarrassments, sick-filled parties, awful love poetry and green condoms, Kelly Ann is a hilariously endearing character. *My Now or Never Diary* is the eagerly awaited sequel.

Corgi Books 0 552 55332 8
978 0 552 55332 2 (from January 2007)

Corgi Books 0 552 55334 4
978 0 552 55334 6 (from January 2007)

Ros Asquith

LOVE, FIFTEEN

Amy ~~AMARYLLIS~~ BAKER: HER DIARY

In Which Amy's Life Is Over,
And That's Just the Beginning . . .

The pregnancy test is called Herald. Great! Blow the trumpets! Hang out the flags! Hold the front page! The chicken has come home to roost! A Little Bundle of Joy is on the way! They should call it Tenterhooks. Or Tough Luck. Or You Are Not Alone . . .

I blame the Turbo Shaglauncher cocktails – Stanley Maul was helping me to drown my sorrows after the love of my life emigrated to Japan, and I have a funny feeling (though I can't seem to remember a thing about it) that he may have given me more than just a mauling . . . Tharg! I've betrayed Tom and now my life is over . . .

Isn't it?

From the bestselling author of the hilarious Teenage Worrier series:

'A female Adrian Mole . . . a mine of information and fun' *Daily Mail*

'Extremely amusing' *Time Out*

Corgi Books 0 552 14777 X
978 0 552 14777 4 (from January 2007)

Unsuitable for younger readers

Expand your mind with these other fantastic reads . . .

Award-winning first book in the acclaimed and powerful trilogy

A true-life story of a teenage girl's battle with anorexia

'Jacqueline Wilson at her very best'
Publishing News

'Agonizingly funny'
Girl's Life magazine

Available from all good booksellers or online at

www.kidsatrandomhouse.co.uk